Also by Saylor Storm

Dr. Selfish (Arnie Darrow series)

With Malicious Intent (Arnie Darrow series)

Double Down (Arnie Darrow series)

Uncorked (Arnie Darrow series)

"The world's greatest power is the youth and beauty of a woman."
- Chanakya

Saylor Storm

Sue's Seduction

A Novel

Sue's Seduction is a work of fiction. Names, characters, places and incidents are either a product of the author's imagination or are used fictitiously. Any resemblance to actual persons, living or dead, events, or locals is entirely coincidental unless you are suffering from delusions of grandeur.

Originally published on my ink jet printer for my editor to tear apart.

Dedication

To John Phelan who has helped me through this process from the very beginning. Thank you for your technical support and for the enticing book covers. Best wishes for your success on your new life's path.

Chapter 1

Free radicals in the body can damage healthy cells.

Sue slowly came into consciousness. The dark room gradually became familiar as she looked around her bedroom through blurred eyes. Her mouth was dry, and she opened it several times tasting the cigarettes from the night before.

She moved onto her side feeling an ache in her back and in her hip. She contemplated getting out of bed, but what for? She didn't have much to look forward to. She decided to get up and wearily pull herself through another day.

Sue dragged herself into the bathroom, and looked at herself in the mirror with one eye open. Ugh! Is that really me in the mirror, where did that bag come from? And, there's another wrinkle!

She stood sideways, evaluating the large paunch that was impossible to ignore. What was she going to do about that? She told herself that she would go to the gym after work. It would come off eventually.

Shuffling to the kitchen, she started a pot of coffee and turned on "Good Morning America". She added a dollop of vanilla flavored creamer. Her day was starting to look a little better.

She looked around for something to eat for breakfast and she spotted some stale cookies on the counter. She ate two and told herself that she would work them off in the gym later.

She took a quick shower, and then tried to decide what to wear. This was the most depressing part of her day. She was down to only three or four items in her closet that fit her. She opted for a blue and black silk oversized top, black leggings and a pair of black flats.

She did a quick onceover of her short, black hair with the blow dryer. A little pink blush, some mascara, and a little lip-gloss. Ready, she headed out the door, first stopping for a second cup of coffee in a to-go cup.

Once inside her white sedan, she turned on the news, listening half-heartedly during the short fifteen minute drive to her office.

Mindlessly, she made herself at home at the same desk where she had worked for the past 12 years. Being a receptionist for a law firm was not exactly her dream, but it paid the bills.

There was a pile a messages on her desk, one from her ex-husband, John. What did he want this time? She decided to call him back first and get it out of the way.

"I'm getting tired of this, Sue," he started.

Sue rolled her eyes. "What are you tired of, John?"

"Your games, Sue. We have a legal arrangement and I certainly expect for you to stick to that agreement."

"Okay, John, what else?"

"Nothing, just do what you're supposed to do."

"Goodbye, John."

She hung up the phone wishing that John would vanish from her life. He had everything, after all: a young wife, money, and nice trips. Why couldn't he just leave her alone?

She sat down at her computer, and did a Google search for anti-aging. A list of articles came up; one in particular caught her eye. It was an ad asking for volunteers to be part of a long-term anti-aging product testing. She immediately filled out the long application form and went back to the work on her desk.

Chapter 2

Antioxidants can have a profound effect in delaying the aging process.

Mid-morning, Sue snacked on a donut and another cup of coffee. It was only 11:00 and she was dragging. Lunch was a serving of chicken strips and a diet coke.

The end of the workday finally arrived and the last thing she wanted to do was head to the gym, but she did. She completed 30 minutes on the treadmill and a few upper body exercises, stopping frequently to chat with fellow exercisers.

She unenthusiastically drove herself home, and poured herself a large glass of wine the moment she walked through the door.

She sat in front of the television and got caught up on the news. The phone rang. She and her friend, Margie, chatted about the latest gossip for a half hour, then she poured another glass of wine and heated up a lean cuisine meal in the microwave.

Her favorite reality shows were on and she watched happily, as she ate a large bowl of ice cream before going to bed. Her sleep was light and interrupted. She awakened feeling unrested and started the whole process over again.

She was back in the office when her cell phone rang.

"May I speak to Susan Kent, please?" the woman asked.

"This is Susan."

"I'm calling from Second Spring Ceuticals. You filled out a form on line yesterday?"

"Yes," Sue answered.

"You are a perfect candidate for our trial. Are you still interested?"

"Well, yes. I am," Sue said.

"Would you be willing to come to our offices for further testing?"

"Yes. Where are you?" Sue asked.

"Here in Reno. We have an office on Mill Street. Could you come in on Saturday?" the woman asked.

"Yes, what time?" Sue inquired.

Susan arrived at the laboratory fifteen minutes late. She was immediately escorted to meet a physician. He was in his late forties and slender, with fair skin and thin, light gray hair. His long, oval face was offset by a pair of thin wire-rimmed rectangular glasses.

"Nice to meet you, Susan. I'm Dr. Elmhurst," he said. "We are excited that you are here. We think that our program is perfect for you."

"I really don't know much about your program. Please tell me about it, Doctor."

"Our research is about to change the world, and we think that you can be part of one of the most exciting medical studies that we will see in our lifetime. We believe that we have a product that will reverse the aging process; it will eventually make it possible to live forever."

Sue raised her eyebrow. "How do I fit in?"

"We would like you to be one of the first fortunate people to benefit from our product. We will ask you to take one capsule per day for the next three years. This is a long-term clinical trial. We will be following you closely. It's completely safe."

"All I have to do is take a pill?" she asked, doubtfully.

"Yes, and we will be testing you frequently. We will also ask for your 100% discretion. You will not be able to tell anyone about our program. It's extremely important that you keep this to yourself. You will have the benefit of turning back the clock. We expect that you will soon have the body and mind that you had as a 20 year old."

Her mind wandered to the image of herself as a svelte cocktail waitress in a skimpy uniform. She looked down at her giant belly.

"It's perfectly safe?" she asked.

"Yes, completely."

"Where do I sign?"

Dr. Elmhurst handed Sue a non-disclosure form to sign.

"We have much work to do. Let's get started. Please put on this gown. The base line tests will take several hours."

"When do I start on the pills?" she asked.

"As soon as we're done here today."

Sue smiled.

Chapter 3

In 2005, 1 out of every 2 Americans had at least one
chronic illness.

Sue spent the entire day at the clinic. They took 10 vials
of blood, gave her a stress test, an electrocardiogram, took
her temperature, blood pressure, weight. They tested her
body fat and gave her balance and coordination tests. She
spent two hours answering written questions about her
habits, moods and emotions. They even took pictures of
her face, hands and body. At the end of all of this, she was
exhausted.

Dr. Elmhurst gave her a bottle of pills before she
departed.

"Remember, Sue, just one pill a day. We'll see you in a
week, and remember, don't tell anyone about this. If you
do, I'm afraid we will have to drop you. I'm sorry, but we
need complete discretion."

"I understand, Doctor. I'll see you next week."

Sue pulled the bottle out of her purse the moment she sat in the car. She took off the cap and shook a red pill into her hand, and then she grabbed a watered down cup of diet coke and took a big swig, washing the pill down.

She called her friend, Margie, on the way home.

"Are we going out tonight?" she asked.

"The usual," Margie answered. "Everyone is coming tonight. See you at six."

Sue stared at the clothes in her closet, trying to decide what she might wear tonight. She was tired of wearing the same old things, but she certainly did not want to go shopping until she lost some weight! Finally, she grabbed her "going out" uniform: a flowing black tunic, black pants and lots of silver jewelry to detract attention from her body.

She was late, as usual, as she pulled up to Rum Bullions at the Silver Legacy in time for happy hour with her regular group of girlfriends. Saturday night was always the same: cosmopolitans, pizza, and gossip about everyone in town. This night, though there were too many cocktails, so the group shared a cab home. Upon arriving, Sue grabbed a couple of cookies before heading off to bed to watch television.

Sunday morning was her time to sleep in. She felt refreshed as she opened her eyes and glanced around the room. She had slept through the night and that didn't happen very often.

She rolled out of bed and stopped by the bathroom to splash some cold water on her face. She didn't look as bad as she thought she would after a night on the town.

She drank her coffee and wondered what to have for breakfast. A bran muffin sounded good.

Then she had a sudden urge to go to the gym. She managed an extra ten minutes on the treadmill and opted for eight pound weights instead of the usual five.

When she got home, instead of watching movies, Sue decided to clean out her guest room, which had been piled with clothes and junk for months. It felt good to clear the clutter.

Her daughter, Karen, called, "How are you, Mom?"

"I'm fine. Everything's good."

"Dad says that you've been causing problems again."

"Oh, you know you're father. He's always complaining about me."

"Mom, you really need to behave. It's not his fault that he's moved on with his life and you haven't."

Sue sighed heavily. "Okay, Dear, I'll try."

She hung up the phone, feeling exasperated and depressed, so she went to the refrigerator, opened a bottle of wine and lit a cigarette. She fell asleep in front of the TV.

Chapter 4

Among the countries of the world, Italy has the highest number of adults over 65.

Sue awakened early Monday morning. She had slept through the night once again.

She took her red pill with a cup of coffee, and then she ran a load of laundry, made her bed, and unloaded the dishwasher before leaving for work.

Her mood was high, so she turned on some music instead of listening to the usual news and she found herself humming and moving to the music in her seat.

When she arrived at the office, there was another message from John on her desk. She returned his call.

"What's up?" she asked cheerfully.

"I'm just checking on you. Karen said you sounded depressed."

"Do I sound depressed?" she chirped.

"No…you don't," he said, sounding surprised.

"Anything else then?"

"No, I guess not."

"See ya!"

Sue hung up the phone and happily went about her day. She had been looking forward to going to the gym after work. Once there, her pace on the treadmill quickened, and she added another 15 minutes to her time. Then, refreshed, she returned home to vacuum and dust before heading to the kitchen for a glass of wine.

The week flew by, and on Saturday she was back at Dr. Elmhurst's clinic.

"How are you feeling, Sue?" he asked.

"Pretty good, Doctor."

He listened thoughtfully. "We'll do some more blood work today to see how you're progressing. First, I want to test you on the treadmill, and there are more questionnaires for you to fill out."

Sue dutifully followed the doctor's instructions and she was sent home with another week's worth of red pills. She met the girls for drinks at the usual spot.

"Can we talk about something other than gossip?" she asked.

The other women looked at her, wordless.

"C'mon, let's have some fun. Let's play fantasy. Let's talk about where we want to go, what we want to do with our lives, what our dreams are!" she said enthusiastically.

"Sue, I've known you for 20 years, and I've never heard you utter a word about your dreams. What's gotten into you?"

"I don't know. I just thought it would be fun to do something different tonight."

The women ignored Sue and resumed their own conversation as though there had been no interruption.

Chapter 5

Every 29 minutes an older adult dies following a fall.

Sue was feeling pretty good; she had been on the pills for two weeks. It was time for her second follow-up with Dr. Elmhurst.

"So, what changes have you noticed, Sue?" he asked.

"Well, the first thing that I noticed, Doctor, is that I started sleeping through the night right away. Then my energy increased, pretty much from the first pill. Later I noticed that a cut on my leg that had been there for months just disappeared. My hair is getting curly and my nails are growing like weeds."

"That's very interesting, Sue. Anything else?"

"Those are the main things."

"Okay, we'll see you in two weeks." He handed her two weeks' worth of pills.

"Thanks, Doctor."

Sue continued to build more energy over the next two weeks. She was sleeping better, working out more, and junk food had lost its appeal.

Her skin was clearer and her eyes brighter. She noticed that her clothes were all becoming loose and her improved mood was becoming noticeable to everyone.

Her children were worried that she was on some sort of mood elevator. Her co-workers found her pleasant to be around, and her friends found her to be annoying.

Men were beginning to pay attention to her at the gym and at Rum Bullions on Saturday nights. Everyone wondered what was going on with Sue.

After a month on the pills, Dr. Elmhurst shared with Sue her latest test results and compared them to the first. Sue was dumbfounded. Everything had improved...vastly.

"You are becoming younger, Sue. Here is the proof."

"Is this real, Doctor?"

"Yes, it is. You are becoming younger every day."

Sue had become excited about her life. She would never again be the fat, lonely, depressed, aging woman. That was now in her past. She had nothing but good things to look forward to.

Chapter 6

As women age, they tend to get more wrinkles than men
because men have a thicker dermis.

Sue bounced out of bed every morning, anxious to see
the changes in her face and body. Her wrinkles were
becoming fainter, and the age spots were vanishing. Her
hair was becoming thicker and growing at an alarming
rate. None of the clothes in her closet fit anymore.

She traded "Good Morning America" for music and
danced around the house every morning while getting
ready for work. She greeted her coworkers with a smile
and was bringing baskets of fresh fruit for the office. The
highlight of her day was going to the gym. She signed up
for Zumba, spinning and Jazzercise.

She came home one night, dripping with perspiration,
from one of her classes. Her children were waiting for her,
seated solemnly in her living room.

"Hi guys," she greeted them cheerfully.

Karen and Kevin exchanged a look.

"Mom, what is going on?" Karen started.

"What do you mean?" Sue responded innocently.

"You're not acting like yourself, Mom. Are you on drugs?" Kevin wanted to know.

"Drugs? What would ever make you think that? Can't I just be happy?"

"But, why are you happy? You've never been happy before. Do you have a boyfriend?"

"No, but that's not a bad idea," she said.

"Mom! That's not funny!" Karen exclaimed.

"What would be wrong with my having a boyfriend? It was okay for your father to have a young girlfriend."

"Mother! What is happening to you? We're worried. You look different and act so strange," Kevin said.

"I know, isn't it great?" Sue said, smiling.

The children exchanged another look.

"Okay, Mother. You don't want to talk about it. Just know that we're keeping an eye on you," Kevin exclaimed as he headed for the door.

"Have a nice day, children," Sue said as she opened her front door and kissed each child on the cheek on their way out.

Chapter 7

The number of people aged 80 years old and older will have almost quadrupled to 395 million between 2000 and 2050.

Saturday morning Sue took off to the gym for a Zumba class, and then headed to the mall to buy some news clothes. Her usual size 16 was now a loose 12. She bought up a storm. Sue hadn't worn a size 12 in six years!

She stopped in the local salon to have her hair trimmed and styled. A mani-pedi was in order as well. Sue showed up at Rum Bullions looking like a million dollars.

"Okay, what is going on, Sue? We want to know your secret. You look like an entirely different person than you did two months ago!" one of the women exclaimed.

"I don't know what you're talking about. I just started exercising a little more, that's all," she answered.

We don't believe you. We think that you're hiding something from us. Do you have a young lover somewhere?"

"You guys are ridiculous. I'm happy and losing weight. You act like I've committed some sort of crime."

The women dropped the subject. They watched enviously as several men came to the table to talk to Sue, ignoring the other women. Sue left the restaurant with a stack of men's phone numbers.

Sunday morning Sue received a call from her ex, John.

"I'd like to meet with you, Sue," John said.

"Okay, John, but what for? We haven't seen each other in months, so why now?" she asked.

"I just need to see you. Meet me for brunch?" he asked.

"Okay, see you in an hour."

Sue admired herself in the mirror as she prepared to meet John. Her skin was glowing, and her wrinkles were a distant memory. She threw on a brightly colored sundress and a pair of sparkly sandals.

She arrived at Rapscallion right on time. John was waiting at one of the outdoor tables.

"Wow! You look incredible," John blurted.

Sue smiled with satisfaction.

"The kids are right. You've made a total transformation." He couldn't take his eyes off of her.

"So, what's going on, John? Why have I been summoned?"

"Well, there are a couple of reasons. First, the kids and I are worried about you."

"That's just ridiculous," she interjected.

"The second reason is that I'm having issues with Brittany and was hoping for some advice."

John now had Sue's full attention. "Issues? What kind of issues?"

"She just doesn't understand me. She's spending so much money and now she wants a baby!"

Sue smirked with satisfaction. "You want my advice?"

"Yes, please. You have always been so level headed and I value your opinion."

"As you can see, your first concern is moot. I am totally fine. Everyone needs to stop freaking out just because I'm happy. As for the second point, really, John, what would you expect me to say? You married a younger woman. This is the price. Pay up or get out."

"But, Sue," John interjected.

"No buts, John. You asked for my opinion and I gave it to you. Now eat your lunch." Sue was pleased with her new position of power over John.

Chapter 8

10% of all persons diagnosed with HIV/Aids are over 50 years of age.

   Sue had finally decided to take the plunge and go out with several of the men who had asked her out at Rum Bullions. She hadn't been on a date since she had dated John…twenty-five years earlier. She was nervous and confident at the same time.

   Her first date was with a fifty-something stockbroker. She found him to be attractive and intelligent. They met at her favorite Rum Bullions on Tuesday night. He bought her a couple of drinks and they made out in his car for two hours afterward. Her date tried to push things further, but Sue wasn't quite ready…yet.

   Sue's confidence, however, was building with each date. She went dancing with the next one, a middle aged insurance salesman. She laughed the night away, but still wasn't ready for the big step yet.

After a couple of weeks of dating, she made her choice and invited her potential partner to her home for dinner. Sue prepared a simple meal of steaks and baked potatoes. They started with martinis...two each. Her date, the stockbroker, didn't take long to make his move.

They were sitting on her sofa when his hands began to wander under her dress. It had been years since she had felt the touch of a man. He forcefully pursued his intention, quickly exposing her breasts, fondling them and placing them in his mouth.

Sue felt like exploding then and there. Her date yanked her dress up around her thighs and followed with his hands. In one quick pull, he managed to remove her lace panties.

He quickly unzipped his pants and mounted his eager partner. Sue tried to be silent as he swiftly entered her. The event was not long lasting, but it was long enough to remind her of what she had been missing.

Sue did not see the man again. She chose to have several more one-night stands and was surprised by the variety of her lovers. They provided her with experiences that she never had with John. Her ex-husband had never performed oral sex on her, something that she found herself enjoying very much.

Sue became insatiable over the next months, feeling that she had years to make up for in the bedroom. She dated several men, some for weeks, others a few months.

She was continuing to feel younger and sexier with each passing day. The offers from men increased as well. She was dating men who were younger and younger.

Her children were less than happy with her newfound lifestyle. They were convinced that their mother had somehow lost her mind. They could not, however, explain her improved looks and attitude.

Chapter 9

Recent studies show that more than 70% of men and women continue sexual activity after 65 years.

Sue went to Dr. Elmhurst's clinic for her six-month evaluation.

"So, tell me, Sue, how are things going for you?" he asked.

"I feel amazing, Dr. Elmhurst. I feel like a girl again, and I even look like one. I have energy; I'm happy. My gray hair and wrinkles are completely gone. My waistline is back and I feel sexy. I even started my period again! I went through menopause 10 years ago!"

"You were 55 when you first came in here, and according to all of your tests, you have the body of a forty year old. You will continue to grow younger the longer that you take the pill. In the meantime, continue to take your daily pill, and I want to see you again in a month. By the way, you had better get on some sort of birth control if you don't want to have another child at this point in your life."

What a bizarre concept that was: having a baby at 55, while her other children were already grown!

Sue stopped on the way home to buy more new clothes at her favorite store, B's Boutique. Her size twelves had to be traded in for size eights. The salesclerk started a conversation with Sue.

"Haven't I seen you in here before?" she asked while moving her head from side to side.

"Yes, I was in here a few months ago," Sue responded.

"Did you lose some weight?" she asked.

"Yes, quite a bit."

"I remember you now. You look amazing! Let me get you some more revealing clothes to show off your new body."

The woman returned with two large handfuls of clothes on hangers. "Here, start with these," she instructed.

Sue went into the dressing room while the woman waited outside the door.

"Do you mind if I ask how old you are?" the woman asked.

"I'm 55."

"No way!"

"It's true. I can show you my driver's license."

"You'll have to tell me your secret. You're the youngest-looking 55-year-old that I've ever seen."

Sue chose several outfits with the help of the salesclerk.

"Here's my card. Please let me know if you need anything."

Sue gave her one of her cards as well. "Thank you for your help today. It was a pleasure."

Sue turned the music up in her little white sedan and opened the window to feel the wind in her hair. She was feeling quite pleased with her life and her appearance.

She met the girls at the usual spot. She looked sexy in her new short skirt, blouse with cut out shoulders and high-heeled silver sandals. She curled her now long black hair into ringlets. Everyone in the bar turned to look as she entered.

"Good God, Sue! When are you ever going to stop losing weight and looking younger? This is getting ridiculous!" Margie said.

Sue just smiled as she took a seat. A young man appeared at her side and asked her to dance. Sue disappeared to the dance floor, not returning for an hour. Her friends were not pleased.

Another man came to the table, and Sue danced the night away. Her friends were green with envy.

"I'm calling her daughter tomorrow," Margie said. "Something just isn't right here. It must be drugs. How else could she have lost so much weight so fast?"

"I'll bet she's had plastic surgery too." One of the women chimed in.

Sue returned to her friends before the evening was over. She had collected several phone numbers from her dance partners.

Chapter 10

Older females exhibit better health care practices than older males.

Sunday afternoon, Sue received a call from the salesclerk at her favorite boutique.

"I've talked to my boss about this already," she began. Sue was curious.

"We've been looking for a model and we think you would be perfect."

Sue was flattered.

"It wouldn't pay anything, but you would get some free clothes."

"I would love to," Sue said without hesitation.

"Great. Stop by the store sometime this week and we'll talk about it."

"Thank you," Sue said.

Can my life get any better, she wondered? Young men, modeling, it was all working out so well.

The phone rang again. It was John.

"What's up?" she asked.

"I need to see you. May I come over?"

"What's this about?" she asked.

"I'm having problems with Brittany. I need to talk to you."

"Okay, come on over," she responded reluctantly.

Sue was dressed in a skintight bright pink workout suit when John arrived. Her hair was still curled from the night before.

John made a sound of surprise as Sue answered the door. "You look fantastic," he said.

"Thank you. Come in. Can I get you anything?" she asked.

"No, thanks. I just need to talk to you."

"Let's sit in the living room," she suggested.

"What's going on?" she asked with a look of concern."

"I can't stop thinking about you," John said.

"What are you talking about?" Sue asked.

"I'm absolutely obsessed with you. I have to have you back. I made a huge mistake. Can you forgive me?" John asked.

"What about Brittany? Your marriage?" Sue inquired.

"It was all a huge mistake. It's you that I've loved all along," he said.

John made his move, grabbing his ex-wife with both arms and forcing her to kiss him.

Her mind was racing. She used to fantasize about this. But is that what she wanted now? What the hell…

She let herself go and kissed him back. Five minutes later they were naked in her bed. He couldn't stop talking, "I've missed you so much. I want you back. You know that we're right together."

25

Sue didn't utter a word; she just tried to absorb the strange situation.

They made love and it was as if no time had passed. John's lovemaking was exactly as it had been years earlier. However, Sue wasn't the same anymore.

John spent the night with his arms wrapped tightly around his ex-bride. He hadn't held her like that since they were newlyweds. This was her dream come true. How many times had she wished that he would come back? Here he was.

Sue lay awake most of the night, her mind racing. What was she going to do?

They made love again in the morning, had coffee together, and Sue fixed bacon and eggs, just like she had always done before.

"John, I really need to get to work. I'm going to be late."

"Can I see you tonight?" he asked eagerly.

"I have a spin class tonight. I'll talk to you later."

Sue quickly closed the door behind him. She let out a deep sigh.

Chapter 11

Older adults are less anxious about death than younger and middle-aged adults.

Sue stopped at the boutique on her way home from work. They asked her to try on several pieces of clothing. The owner chose several for Sue to wear in an upcoming fashion show.

Karen was waiting for her when she got home.

"What's all that?" Karen asked.

"Just some clothes from B's."

"More clothes, Mother? Didn't you just buy some last week?"

"I did. They gave these to me."

"Gave them to you? What for?"

"I'm modeling for the store now," Sue said factually.

"You're what? Modeling? This is not the mother that I know. What happened to her?"

"I would think that you would be proud of me, Karen. Would you rather that I go back to the fat, depressed person that I was?"

"Of course not. I just don't understand…"

"I know you don't. It's confusing. I don't really understand it myself."

Sue hugged her daughter.

"I'm scared, Mom. It's like I don't know who you are anymore."

"I'm still the same person, just a little thinner and happier than before. Please, just be happy for me, Karen. Is that asking too much?"

"No, Mom, I guess not."

She hugged her daughter again. "Now, go home and stop worrying about me."

As Sue dressed for her spin class, her phone rang. It was John. She ignored the call.

Spin class was full. Sue loved the loud music, and the energy that pulsed through her body as she rode. She was addicted to the feeling of endorphins.

A young man struck up a conversation with Sue as the class was ending.

"Some of us are going for a drink after class. Would you like to join us?" he asked.

Sue found the man to be attractive and a bit on the young side. She agreed to go.

She threw her pink sweat suit on over her spin shorts and followed the man to the bar.

"I'm Mark, by the way," he said, extending his hand to Sue after they were seated at the table with the others.

"Sue, nice to meet you," Sue responded.

"I've noticed you in class before. You're a very attractive woman, Sue. What you do?"

"I work in a law office. I'm not a lawyer or anything, just an assistant."

"I would have pegged you for a model," he said.

"Well, I am doing a little of that on the side."

"You should be doing more than just a little."

"What do you do, Mark?"

"I'm a personal trainer, studying to be a doctor," he said.

"You certainly are in great shape. Do you mind if I ask how old you are?"

The waitress came and they each ordered a glass of wine.

"I'm 35," he said.

"You're so young," she said staring at his face.

"You must be about the same age," he said matter of factly.

"Yeah, something like that," she answered.

There was no way that she was going to tell him that she was 55!

"Would you like to meet me at the gym tomorrow after work? We could work out together," Mark asked.

"That sounds like fun," Sue answered.

They finished their wine and Sue excused herself from the group.

"I need to get home, " she said. "See you tomorrow."

Sue had turned her phone off before spin class. There were four messages from John.

Once home, she returned his call.

"What's so important?" she asked.

"I have to see you." He said.

"You're a married man, John. Maybe last night was a mistake."

"What? How could you say that? Last night was incredible, the best sex of my life," John said.

Sue was most surprised. How could that possibly be, she wondered?

"John, I need to go now. Go be with your wife. I'll talk to you tomorrow." Sue ended the conversation.

Sue poured herself a big glass of wine and turned on the TV. Her life was beginning to seem complicated.

Chapter 12

People aged 65 currently make up 13 percent of the population.

Sue met Mark at the gym after work. They worked out hard with the weights, both dripping wet as a result.

"How about some dinner?" Mark asked.

"Sure, something casual since we're in our workout clothes."

"I know just the place," he said.

They took Mark's silver Mazda MX-5 to Sup and sat at one of the outside tables. The food was healthy and they ordered a glass of wine.

"I don't know anything about you, Sue. Please fill me in," he asked, interested.

She had to think about this. How would she explain that she had a 20-year-old and a 23-year-old when he thought that she was only 35?

"I'm divorced," she started.

"What happened?" he asked.

"He cheated," she stated flatly. She couldn't tell him that it was with a younger woman. She was now physically younger than Brittany.

"There's really not much to tell. I'd rather hear about you."

Mark filled her in on the essentials.

What was she doing with the gorgeous young man? How would she explain her real age? Her children?

She continued to see Mark every day. They met at the gym and went out to restaurants together.

She was afraid to invite him to her home. What if her kids showed up? Her friends? Or John? She hid the pictures of the kids and invited him over for dinner. She was a nervous wreck.

Their sex life was unbelievable, Sue thought. It had been 20 years since she had been with a man Mark's age. He had incredible drive and stamina.

Their first night together, Mark commented on her pubic hair. "That's so old school," he said, looking at the mound of dark hair between her legs. Sue was embarrassed. "Why don't you have a Brazilian like everyone else?" he asked. Sue made an appointment the following morning.

Their time together focused on fitness. They worked out with weights, took exercise classes and ate at healthy restaurants..

She continued to look younger and more vibrant every day. Sue invited Mark to her fashion show. She was proud to have such a young, handsome man there to support her.

"You were fabulous up there," he stated, proudly. "You should be doing this full time."

"I don't know about that," she said.

"You should think about it. I swear, you get more beautiful by the day." He kissed her.

Chapter 13

Only five percent of the over-65 population lives in
nursing homes.

Margie had been calling Sue every day.

"Why don't we see you anymore? You haven't been to
Rum Bullions in weeks."

"I'm just busy, that's all, Margie, nothing more."

"Karen told me about your modeling. Why didn't you
tell us about it? Are you too good for us now?"

"Don't be ridiculous."

"You might want to show you're friends that you still
exist; that is, if you even care about your friends
anymore," Margie complained.

"Of course I do," Sue said.

Sue was receiving similar treatment from her children
and John. John was not giving up. He called her every day,
pleading for Sue to take him back.

She received a call from the boutique. "The owner and I have been talking," the girl said, "and we want you to be part of our national campaign. It would be a full time job, and the money is really, really good."

Sue was dumbfounded.

"I'll get back to you on Monday. Thank you for the offer," Sue said. She needed time to think things through.

She was due for monthly check-up with Dr. Elmhurst. She couldn't wait to see him. There was no one else for her to talk to.

"You look fantastic, Sue," he commented immediately.

"Thank you, Doctor, but I'm feeling a bit stressed out," she said nervously.

"That's to be expected. Let's take care of your vitals, then we'll talk. You've lost 50 pounds, Sue. That's amazing!"

"I know, Doctor; I feel great."

"You are steadily getting younger, Sue. You are now the equivalent of a 35-year-old."

"Is there any way that we can keep me at 35?" she asked.

"That wasn't our agreement, Sue."

"I know. It's just that my life is getting so complicated..."

"We have an in-house therapist here for you to talk to. You may see her as often as you like, no charge. What you are going through is very common for our participants."

"Thank you, Dr. Elmhurst. I really do need to talk to someone."

"You may go in and talk to her as soon as we're finished here."

Dr. Elmhurst introduced Sue to the therapist. "Call me Shelby," she said, extending her hand. "It's so nice to meet you."

Sue found Shelby to be friendly. She looked to be in her early 30's with blond hair and a cute figure. She was dressed professionally in a dress, heels and black-framed glasses.

"Please, let's step into my office," she suggested. "Dr. Elmhurst filled me in a little. It's very common to have issues and anxieties during this trial. Your life has changed completely."

"Please feel confident that anything you say in here will not be shared. I want you to be completely up-front with me."

"Thank you, Shelby. I will do my best."

"So, why don't you start from the beginning?" the therapist suggested. "We can have sessions every day until we're caught up with your current life."

"I guess I should start where the trial began. I was 55, fat and lonely. My husband had dumped me for a much younger woman; my children treated me like I was a nuisance; my friends were only happy cutting other people down and I placated myself with food, alcohol and cigarettes."

"I really didn't have much of a reason to get up in the morning, and I certainly didn't have anything positive to offer anyone in my life."

"This trial of your product has changed my entire life. Even my ex-husband wants me back now."

"I want to talk about that next time," Shelby said. "I'm making a note of it, but I don't see the problem. Everything sounds wonderful."

"It is...but it isn't. It's just getting so complicated," said Sue.

"Let's save that for next time as well. For now, I want you to focus on all of the positive changes that have occurred since you started on the trial," Shelby suggested. "I want you to make a list of all of the positive changes that have occurred in your life since starting on the product, and I want you to look at the list every day."

"Thank you, Shelby, I will do that," said Sue.

"Before you leave today, I would like you to fill out this questionnaire. We want to measure your levels of anxiety, depression, sleep patterns, etc. Your health is our number one concern and we want to make sure that everything is going smoothly for you, both physically and emotionally," Shelby said.

Sue filled out the one-page form and handed it back to her therapist.

"You will need to fill one of these out every time that you come in, so we can track your progress," Shelby added.

"No problem," said Sue.

"See you tomorrow, Sue."

Sue left feeling a little better about things.

Chapter 14

Families provide 70-80% of the in-home-care for the elderly.

Sue went home that night and turned off her phone. She took a hot bubble bath and tried not to think about her current strange life.

Relaxed and refreshed, she turned up all the lights in her bathroom. She gave herself a thorough visual examination. It was truly astonishing! Her body was nearly perfect, not a mark on it, and the cellulite had completely vanished.

Her breasts were perky once again. Her buttocks were firm and tight and with all of the exercise, she was in better shape now than she had been when she was young.

She pulled out the vanity mirror and looked closely at her face. There were no lines or red marks and her skin was plump.

She ran her hands through her hair. It had grown to her mid-back over these months. It was thick and shiny. There was no trace of gray anymore.

This is truly a miracle, she thought. She smiled. Pleased with her new body, she wrapped herself in her robe.

Feeling better, she turned on her phone. There were 10 messages…all the usual: John, the kids, Margie and Mark.

She texted everyone, saying that she was tired and going to bed early.

She turned on some music, poured herself a glass of wine and pulled out a book. She noticed that she no longer needed her reading glasses.

Sue went to see Shelby the next day on her lunch hour.

"Let's talk about your ex," Shelby started.

"I was thirty when we married. He was successful, attentive and handsome. I guess it's the typical story. I started losing interest in him when the kids came along. I guess I let myself go, too."

"I was a cocktail waitress in a men's club when I met him. I had an adorable figure then, I guess I was what you might call 'perky'."

"He pursued me relentlessly. I fell hard. We were married within the year. We were really happy for the first few years."

"So tell me about the affair?" Shelby asked.

"It was humiliating. Brittany was his secretary. She's twenty years younger, perfect figure, no kids. It was a real reality check for me to realize how much I had stopped caring about our marriage, about myself."

"I became a real pain in the neck for John and Brittany. I couldn't compete, so I decided to make their life as difficult as possible. It was pretty childish. Looking back on it now, I'm pretty ashamed."

"Our poor kids were caught in the middle. No wonder they never wanted to spend any time with me. I was really awful. I'm sure that's how I ended up being so all alone and miserable. Heck, I couldn't even stand my own company!"

"I think that we've made some real progress here today. Call me whenever you want the next appointment," Shelby said. "Please fill out the form before you leave."

"I will. Thank you, Shelby."

Sue drove home thinking about her conversation with Shelby. She had never formed those thoughts into words. It felt good. She never wanted to be that dreadful, immature person again!

The next morning, she called the boutique right away. She had forgotten to call them on Monday.

"I'm so sorry," she apologized. "I would love the job! When do I start?"

Chapter 15

Living below or near the poverty line is a significant problem for most older adults.

Sue called Mark right away.

"I got the job," she spoke hurriedly.

"The job?" he asked.

"Yes, I'm now a full time model, just like you suggested."

"Congratulations! That's great. I told you that's what you should be doing. Let's celebrate tonight. I'll pick you up at seven?"

"Sounds great!"

Sue went to work and gave her two-week notice. They were sorry to see her go. She had recently become an asset to the office.

She had an appointment with Shelby after work.

"I'd like for us to talk about your feelings about your ex," Shelby started.

"Okay, but first I wanted to tell you that I got a new job today, as a full-time model. Can you believe it?"

"You're a beautiful woman. Why not?" Shelby asked.

"No one had given me the time of day months ago, and now I'm a model! It's just so unbelievable! They all think that I'm the best looking thing they've ever seen and all I have to do to look this way is to take a little red pill every day. If they only knew!"

"Don't you think that you deserve to be a model?" Shelby asked.

"I don't really know. I'm so confused. I love looking like this, and the attention I'm getting, but it's just not right, somehow," Sue said.

"Why do you think that you don't deserve to be happy, Sue?" Shelby asked.

"I haven't done anything to achieve this new life, this new body. I was such an awful person before, and it's as if I'm being rewarded for my bad behavior somehow," Sue said, thoughtfully.

"Everyone deserves to be happy, Sue. Why would you be any different from anyone else?" Shelby asked.

"I guess you're right. I feel as though I need to do something worthwhile with my life, so that I will feel as though I deserve all of these wonderful changes in my life," Sue responded.

"Enjoy your new life, Sue. You deserve it. Be happy. Everyone deserves that, even you," said Shelby.

"Thank you, Shelby. I will try and remember that."

"Don't forget to fill out your form," Shelby reminded Sue. "See you next time, Sue."

Sue rushed home to change for dinner. She wore a skin-tight bright red dress with spiked black shoes. She blew her long, black hair out straight. It reached the top of her buttocks.

Mark arrived, flowers in hand.

"Congratulations, again", he said as he handed her the flowers. "You look absolutely amazing. I swear, you become more beautiful every day."

"Thank you. You are so sweet." She took the flowers.

Her phone rang as they were leaving her house. It was John. She turned off her phone.

"Where are we going?" she asked Mark.

"I thought that we would splurge on a steak at Harrah's Steak House," he said, as he looked her for approval.

"That sounds perfect!"

Mark ordered a couple of dirty martinis as they perused the menu.

Sue felt relaxed and on top of the world. She was now a real model, with a gorgeous, young man at her side. Could it possibly get any better?

They enjoyed their steaks at a leisurely pace. Leaving the restaurant hours later, they walked hand in hand through the casino.

A woman stood in their way.

"Sue?" she asked.

Sue's heart stopped. It was Margie.

"Oh, hi," she said timidly.

"Aren't you going to introduce me?" Margie asked.

"This is Mark," she said, looking at the floor.

Mark held out his hand, "I'm Mark. Nice to meet you," he said confidently.

Margie started to speak, but Sue interrupted her.

"Margie is an old friend of the family."

Margie shook Mark's hand.

"It was nice to see you, Margie, we were just on our way out," Sue said hurriedly.

She grabbed Mark's hand and pulled him towards the door.

"What was that all about?" he asked.

"She is a friend of my mother's. She's a busybody. I just wanted to get away from her."

"Okay, but you are just acting pretty strange."

"It's nothing. Let's go home."

"Does that mean that I get to spend the night this time?"

"Sure, why not?"

She just prayed that no one would show up uninvited.

Once home, she checked her phone. There were four messages from John. He was desperate to see her, and there was a text message from Margie.

A friend of the family? Really? What was that? Who the hell was that man?

She took a deep breath and sent a message to John.

Will talk to you tomorrow.

Then she sent a text to Margie.

I will explain tomorrow. Sorry.

Hopefully, that would be enough to appease everyone for the rest for the night.

Chapter 16

Most older workers are just as effective in their jobs as
younger workers.

Sue managed to get through the night without any
unexpected visitors. She didn't get much sleep worrying
about the possibilities, so she rushed Mark out the door
early.

She turned her phone on at eight and there were already
several messages. She returned the call from the boutique
first.

"Can you come in today, so we can talk?" the manager
asked.

"I'll be by on my lunch hour, if that works," Sue
suggested.

"Great, see you then."

Now that that was out of the way, it was time to make
the dreaded phone call to Margie.

"Well, I'm waiting," Margie said as she answered the phone.

"I'm sorry, Margie. That was an awkward situation. I didn't handle it very well."

"That's for sure. So, who was that guy?" Margie asked.

"He's sort of my boyfriend," Sue stated quietly.

There was silence on the other end of the phone.

"Margie, are you still there?"

"Yes, I'm here," Margie answered.

"Well?" Sue asked.

"Well, what? I have no idea who you are anymore. You have a boyfriend and don't even bother to mention it to your best friend?" Margie answered angrily.

"I didn't think that you would approve," Sue said.

"Why in the world would you care what I think? You don't even talk to me anymore, and then you pretend like you barely know me when you see me," Margie said.

"It's difficult to explain. I'm going through a lot right now," Sue said.

"I'm sorry if you are having a difficult time. It sure looks like you're having the time of your life, but if you care about our friendship, you will make a point of spending some time with me," Margie complained.

"I do care about our friendship. I just need to figure some things out," Sue stated.

"Goodbye, Sue."

"Goodbye."

Sue was relieved to have the conversation over with, but disappointed that it hadn't gone any better. She would talk it over with Shelby during their next session.

Last, but not least, was a phone call to John.

"You've been avoiding me long enough," he complained.

"Come over tonight for dinner and we'll talk," she said.

"Good. See you then," John said.

It felt as if the world were closing in on her.

Chapter 17

40 to 50 percent of Americans who live to age 65 will have skin cancer.

Sue rushed to work, feeling frantic. She raced to B's on her lunch hour.

"We've made out a tentative schedule for you. There will be quite a bit of travel. You will be working fashion shows and photo shoots."

Travel? Perfect, she thought. She needed to get away and think about things.

She shook the manager's hand and promised to show up for the photo shoot the following week.

She raced back to the office. She had time after work to see Shelby before John was due for dinner.

"This is all getting so crazy," Sue said to Shelby. "I feel like I'm dodging one lie after another."

"Calm down. Take a deep breath, and tell me what happened," Shelby suggested.

"Last night I was out with my 35-year-old boyfriend, who no one knows about, by the way, and we ran into my best friend. I couldn't tell him that she was my friend when she looks like she should be my mother and I didn't want her to meet Mark. She'll think that I'm a dirty old woman."

"You didn't do anything wrong, Sue. You just need to figure out your priorities in your life. Everything has changed. Do you want to keep your old friends? Or, do you want to have a life with your new young man?" Shelby asked.

"That's a really good question. I haven't had time to think about any of this. I've just been running. The good thing is that I'm going to start traveling for work. That should give me a little breathing space," said Sue.

"I want you to give some thought to what you really want from your life right now before we meet next time. You have everything at your fingertips. It's your choice," Shelby suggested.

"How are you feeling, by the way? Are you feeling anxious or depressed? How is your sleep?" Shelby asked.

"I guess I'm a little anxious and depressed, but mostly just confused. It feels like I'm not able to please anyone in my life right now."

"Why is it important for you to please everyone else? Isn't it a nice change for you to be thinking about yourself first for once?" Shelby asked.

"I just don't know anymore. I'm so confused," Sue admitted.

"Focus on the positives in your life right now and give some serious thought to what is most important to you. What do want in your life."

"Okay, Shelby. I will do that."

"Don't forget your form, Sue," Shelby reminded her.

"Oh, of course," Sue responded.

Sue drove home feeling more confident about her situation. She felt more relaxed as she stopped to buy groceries for her dinner with John.

John? What was she thinking? He had been relentless in pursuing her. He was probably going to take her invitation as a come-on.

She beat John to the house by 10 minutes.

"Come on in," she said. "Give me a minute to change my clothes."

"Would you put on that little hot pink work out suit again?"

"No, John, I won't. Make yourself a drink. I'll be right out."

She reappeared in a baggy pair of jeans and an oversized sweatshirt. She didn't want to give John the wrong idea.

Sue quickly threw together a stir-fry meal, hoping to get the dinner over with as soon as possible.

"It's wonderful to have you cooking for me again. It's just like old times," he said, looking adoringly at her.

"No, John, it's not like old times. I invited you over tonight to tell you that I'm seeing someone else. Our night together was a mistake."

"Who is he?" he asked.

"It doesn't matter. You and I aren't going to happen, no matter what. I would like for us to be friends, though, for the kids' sake."

"You know that I don't take no for answer. I'm not going to give up."

John stormed out the door.

"Whew! Thank God that's over!" Sue exclaimed.

Sue drew a hot bubble bath and soaked for an hour before going to bed.

Chapter 18

There are more people over age 60 than under age 15.

Sue received a call from Mark as she was getting ready for work.

"I missed you last night," he said.

"I missed you, too," she said.

"Can I see you tonight?" he asked.

"Sure," she answered.

She was afraid to be seen in public with him and afraid to bring him home.

"Why don't we go to your house?" she asked.

"Well, I have a roommate, remember? It's much more private at your house," he said.

"I know, I just thought it would be nice for a change," Sue said.

"Okay, I'll make you dinner. Come on over at seven," Mark suggested.

Sue breathed a sigh of relief.

She breezed through her day, stopping by the gym after work for an hour-long workout. She showered, changed and headed to Mark's.

His apartment was on the second floor. It was a small two-bedroom, with a tiny kitchen and bath. There were weights and exercise equipment everywhere. Posters decorated the walls, and clothes were strewn about. She felt as if she were in her son, Kevin's, apartment.

"I tried to warn you," he said. "I'm living like this so I can save money and finish my medical degree."

"It's fine. Don't worry," she said, looking around. She was mortified.

"Dinner will be ready soon. Would you like a glass of wine?" he asked.

At that moment, the front door opened and Mark's roommate entered with a small group of young women.

"We're here to study. You don't mind, do you?" he asked.

"I'm trying to entertain here," he said, looking at Sue.

"We won't be in the way," the roommate replied.

Mark looked again at Sue. She shrugged her shoulders.

"Fine, just try to keep it down," Mark said.

The group congregated in the small living room while Mark and Sue adjourned to the tiny kitchen table.

Mark had prepared a prepackaged salad with frozen lasagna.

"Sorry, I never really learned how to cook," he said apologetically.

This was a meal that Kevin would have prepared.

Sue listened to the conversation in the next room. The thirty-something year old women were discussing several celebrities…none of whom Sue had ever heard of.

She turned her attention to Mark. "The meal is just fine. Thank you."

Mark talked as Sue focused, once again, on the conversation coming from the next room. She probably looked younger than the women, but she felt ancient as she heard the conversation.

The couple lingered for a few moments before adjourning to Mark's bedroom. They made love, as quietly as possible. Sue needed to use the bathroom, and was embarrassed when she had walk to the other end of the apartment, past the study group, to get to the bathroom.

Sue and Mark slept through the night and Sue quickly slipped out at dawn.

She had plenty of time to think on the drive home. She concluded that she had not felt that awkward and uncomfortable since college. She had managed to avoid everyone in her life by staying at Mark's, but was it worth it? She needed to see Shelby.

Chapter 19

The elderly are the fastest growing age group.

She was the earliest to arrive at the office...a first for Sue. She had made plans with Karen for lunch and didn't want to have to rush back to the office.

The women met at the Cheese Board. They took a table in the back corner.

"Mom, I haven't seen you in two weeks!" Karen exclaimed.

"I know, Honey, I'm sorry. I've been so busy," Sue said.

"So I hear, Mom," Karen said sarcastically.

"What does that mean?" Sue asked.

"I've been talking to Margie," Karen stated flatly,

"Oh, I can only imagine how that went," Sue said.

"Yes, she told me all about your young boyfriend. Really, Mom?"

"So what's the problem? Your father is with a younger woman," Sue retorted.

"We at least got to meet her and know that she exists," Karen snapped back.

"Why do you have to meet Mark? It's not like I'm going to marry him," Sue said.

"Oh, Mother, what a terrible thought!" Karen exclaimed.

A young woman stopped by the table. "Hi, Karen. Is this your sister?" She asked looking at Sue. "You two look so much alike."

"No. This is Sue," Karen said through a forced smile.

"Hi, I'm Melissa, a classmate of Karen's."

"Nice to meet you, Melissa."

"See you in class later," she said to Karen as she walked away.

"Now, do you see, Mother, how ridiculous this has become? People think that you're my sister! I bet your boyfriend looks like he's about 12!"

"I'm sorry, Karen, that my looks make you uncomfortable. I can't help it. I'm not doing anything intentionally to hurt you."

"Are you ever going to tell us what you're doing? Having surgery? Taking drugs?" Karen asked.

"There's nothing to tell. Let's just drop this and have a nice lunch. Tell me what's going on with you," Sue suggested.

Sue returned to work feeling exasperated by her daughter. She called Shelby to make an appointment after work.

"The walls are closing in," she said.

"My boyfriend reminds me of my son; my daughter's friends think that I'm her sister. Everyone is mad at me. No one understands, and I can't tell anyone the truth," Sue said.

"Let me ask you a question, Sue. If you could turn back time, would you? Would you go back to being the same person that you were before the trial?" Shelby asked.

"No, of course not. I didn't like that person. I'm much happier now," Sue answered.

"Then the people in your life are just going to have to accept you the way you are," Shelby said.

"I'm beginning to feel that I don't fit in anywhere. I honestly felt like a den mother at my boyfriend's house the other night. I didn't have a clue what people were talking about. Outside I'm 30, but inside I'm 55. Does that make any sense to you?" Sue asked.

"Of course, it does. All of our trial members go through a similar dilemma. You'll make peace with it. You're just going through a process."

"I want you to make a list of all of the positives about being 30 again, and a list of the negatives. We'll look it over the next time that you come in," Shelby suggested.

"I'll have to think about that. Thanks, Shelby."

Sue filled out her form and handed it to Shelby before leaving.

"I'm a bit concerned, Sue, that your anxiety and depression levels are mounting. I would like you to step-up your workouts this week and see if that helps at all," Shelby suggested.

Sue stopped by the gym for spin class on her way home. She felt much better after an hour of endorphins pulsing through her veins.

She went home to a quiet house. There were no calls, so she went to bed early.

Chapter 20

Nursing homes cost more than $60,000 per patient for a year.

It was time for a follow-up appointment with Dr. Elmhurst.

"How are you feeling, Sue?"

"Great, Doctor. I've never had this much energy in my life! I've been exercising rigorously, something that I never did in the past."

"I'm concerned, however, that this anti-aging is never going to stop. I don't want to be any younger, Doctor."

"Your test results show that your anti-aging is slowing down. We don't know where this will end up. That's why we are doing the trial. You need to stick with us for the entire three years. Physically you are about 30 now, and, as I said, your reverse aging process is slowing down. Let's see where you are in three months."

"I want you to fill out these forms while you're here today. They detail changes in your body, including vision and memory. We're 10 months into the program now, so we need to take some follow up photographs as well."

"I forgot to tell you that my vision has improved. I don't need glasses any more," she added.

"That's wonderful, Sue. I hear that you've been seeing Shelby on a regular basis. How's that going?" he asked.

"It's helping. It's been so difficult to keep all of this a secret from everyone in my life. It makes a big difference to be able to talk to someone who understands what I'm going through," Sue said.

"I'm glad to hear that it's helping. Please continue to see Shelby as often as you like."

"Thank you, Doctor. See you in a few months."

Sue stopped by the gym on her way home. She took a Zumba class and still had the energy to lift some weights.

There was an email from the manager at B's when she got home. It was her travel itinerary for later in the month. She still had a week left at the law office, but would be totally free to travel after that.

The first trip was scheduled for Hawaii. Not a bad place to start, she thought.

She decided to spend the evening at home, alone, to go through her clothes and see if she had anything appropriate for Hawaii.

Her son, Kevin, called to check in. Sue decided not to mention her new job.

Mark called and they made plans to see each other the following night at Sue's house.

Chapter 21

HGH, the human growth hormone, can give you a more youthful appearance, but can cause cancer cells to grow and spread faster.

Sue had prepared a romantic meal for Mark.

"I have an idea," she said. She had his attention.

"I'm scheduled to go to Hawaii in two weeks for a photo shoot. Why don't you come with me? It would be romantic."

Mark smiled, "That's a great idea, Sue. I love it! What are the details?"

"They've booked me at the Hilton Hawaiian Village for a week. I'll have to work during the day, but I'll have the evenings free."

"I've never been to Hawaii. Have you?" Mark asked.

"Yes, when I was first married," she said, without thinking first.

"I forgot that you were married," Mark looked surprised.

"Oh, yeah, I told you about it. Remember?"

How could she possibly explain her 16 year marriage to John and the kids who were seemingly just a few years younger than herself?

"The trip sounds wonderful, Sue. Thank you for asking me to come along."

The couple went to bed early and had a lengthy love making session. Mark was a very attentive lover.

Chapter 22

People in happy marriages tend to live longer.

It was Sue's last week at work. The office decided to throw her a party at Rum Bullions. She invited Margie and the rest of the girls. She was apprehensive about inviting them, but thought it was the right thing to do.

Her co-workers were sorry to see her go. She had become an asset in the office and was pleasant to be around.

Sue took a seat next to Margie.

"Thank you for coming," she said.

"Thanks you for asking. Why are you leaving, anyway?" Margie asked.

Sue hesitated, "I have another job," she said.

"Really? Doing what?" Margie asked.

"Modeling, full time, for B's Boutique chain," Sue answered hesitantly.

Margie was silent for a moment.

"What's wrong now?" Sue asked her friend.

"Modeling? There's no future in that! What are you thinking, Sue? You and I both know how old you are. You're not going to look this good forever."

Sue sighed heavily, "Can't you just be happy for me? This is the dream of a lifetime."

"Whatever," Margie muttered.

Sue left the table and rejoined her coworkers who were much more fun to be around than Margie and the others. Sue enjoyed herself and was happy to be starting a new chapter in her life.

The next morning, there was a call from John.

"I have to see you," he said urgently.

"I don't think that's a good idea. We've been over this, John," she replied.

"You don't understand. I have to see you right away."

Against her better judgment, she agreed.

15 minutes, later, John was knocking on her door. She was busy packing for Hawaii.

"What's all this?" he asked.

"I'm going on a trip. What is it, John?"

"I've left Brittany. I had to show you that I'm serious about us. I'm free now. We can be together."

Sue wanted to burst out laughing, but she knew that she now had a big problem on her hands.

"Nobody asked you to do that, John. I've been very clear with you that I don't want to be with you and that I'm seeing someone else."

"But, I did this for you…for us," John said.

"There is no 'us' anymore John. That ended years ago when you started an affair with Brittany."

Sue walked to the front door and held it open. "Now, if there's nothing else, I have packing to do."

Angered, John stormed through the door. "I'm not giving up!"

Sue took a deep breath and quickly slammed the door. That was the last thing she needed, she concluded.

Chapter 23

Conscientious people live longer.

Sue and Mark left for Hawaii the following morning. They flew out of Reno and changed planes in San Francisco. A driver was waiting for them in Honolulu.

Sue had been to the Hilton Hawaiian Village numerous times with John and the kids when they were little. It looked just the same, and so did she for the most part.

They were upgraded to a suite with an ocean view on the 19th floor of the Tapa Tower.

"This is unbelievable!" Mark exclaimed. "Look at that view! Come here, You!"

Mark grabbed Sue by the waist and forcefully pulled her close, kissing her passionately.

"Wow!" she exclaimed.

"We are going to have the most romantic week ever. This is the perfect place!" He grinned from ear to ear.

They made love and headed to the pool for a swim. Dinner was romantic at the hotel. They went to bed early, making love again.

Sue was picked up at 8:00A.M. She would be shooting at Diamond Head all day.

Mark surfed, worked out at the gym and hung out at the pool. Each day was the same. Sue worked all day, while Mark relaxed. They got together in the evening, had a romantic dinner and made love.

Their last night on the island was, however, a little different. They were having a romantic dinner on the beach at the Royal Hawaiian Hotel.

Mark started, "This has been the most incredible week of my life. I think that you are the most amazing woman, Sue. I've had a lot of time to think this week while you've been working. I've also had time to shop."

He pulled out an open ring box. It had a diamond ring in it. Sue almost fell off of her chair. This was the last thing that she expected.

Chapter 24

In the U.S., Alzheimer's disease effects four million people.

How did this happen, she wondered? How was she going to get out of this one? Marriage had never entered her mind. She couldn't possibly marry Mark. How would she possibly explain her age and her kids? What a mess!

"I've been thinking, Sue. I think that you would make the most amazing mother. I think that we should have two kids, a girl and a boy. What do you think?"

Her head was reeling. This couldn't possibly be happening! Mark was waiting for an answer.

"That's so sweet, Mark. I don't know what to say."

"You're supposed to say 'yes'," he said.

"I don't think I can do that," she said.

"I don't understand. What do you mean?" Mark asked.

"I'm not saying no; I just need a little time to get used to the idea."

"I can't say that I'm not disappointed. I was expecting a different response. Here, wear the ring while you're trying to decide."

He slipped the ring onto Sue's finger. It was enormous.

"Mark, where did you get the money for this? I thought you were saving every penny for school," Sue asked.

"My dad wired me the money. He's a sucker for weddings. He's been married four times. He said I can pay him back after I'm an established physician."

"Wow, I really just don't know what to say."

"Tell me that you love me," he said, holding her hand.

"I do love you, Mark."

Sue was in a full panic. How would she ever get out of this situation? She needed an appointment with Shelby immediately!

Chapter 25

Most adults become happier as they get older.

Sue managed to stall Mark for a while. She had plenty of time to think on the five-hour flight back to San Francisco. She stared at the large, shiny ring on her left finger and came up with a plan.

She asked Mark to give her a week to think about things. That would buy her enough time to implement her plan. Sue paid a visit to the B's store manager.

"Where is the store headquarters located?" she asked.

"It's near Asheville, North Carolina. Why do you ask?"

Perfect! Sue thought. It's far away.

"Do you think it would be a problem if I worked from there from now on?"

"You mean relocate to Asheville?"

"That's exactly what I mean," Sue said.

"Are you kidding? That would be wonderful! We would have you right there at the center of things. We would have a lot more work for you there. Do you mind if I ask why?"

"It's a long story. I just need to relocate," said Sue.

"When do you want to go?"

"I'll be there by the end of the week," Sue informed her.

"The company is going to be thrilled! You look incredible, by the way. Whatever you're doing, keep doing it. I want to know your secret!"

Sue just smiled as she shook the manager's hand before departing.

Sue's mind raced as she drove home. She had a lot to do and a short time to do it in.

She did a Google search on Asheville. It looked like a good place to get lost. She emailed a realtor and told him what she was looking for, and that she would be in town next week.

Sue drove to the Lexus dealership on Mill Street.

"I need something bigger," she said to the salesman, pointing at her small sedan. "I have cash," she added. "Something used, maybe one of those," she said pointing to the lot.

The salesman's eyes lit up. He showed her a used LX 570 for $22,000. She offered him $20,000. An hour, and piles of paperwork later, she drove the car off the lot.

She stopped at a liquor store and loaded the back of the car with empty cardboard boxes. Then she pulled the car into her garage and quickly closed the door behind her. She unloaded the boxes into her bedroom and shut the door.

Just then, Karen pulled up into the driveway.

Oh shit! Sue thought. I don't want her to know what I'm up to, so she took a deep breath and opened the door trying to look as relaxed as possible.

"Hi, Honey, what a nice surprise!" she said, forcing a smile.

"How was Hawaii, Mom? You look better than ever with a tan."

"Oh, it was fabulous. Relaxing, even though I was working." She didn't want Karen to know that Mark had gone with her to Hawaii, so she quickly removed the large diamond ring from her left hand, and stuck it into her pants pocket.

"How are things with you?" Sue changed the subject as fast as possible.

Karen visited for fifteen minutes before Sue made excuses and suggested that she needed to get back to catching up from her trip.

Chapter 26

An unhappy childhood shortens one's life.

Sue packed her favorite clothes, jewelry and cosmetics.
She didn't need much and she wanted to leave the
impression that she would be returning soon. There would
new clothes awaiting her in North Carolina.

She went to the bank, and took out all of her cash. She
had all of her mail forwarded to an arbitrary post office
box in Kansas City. From there, her mail would be
discreetly forwarded to her new address in Asheville.

The following morning, before dawn, Sue was in her car,
headed east to North Carolina. She had five days to think
while driving. Her plan was to disappear for a while, not
for good. She needed time to think, and to breathe. She
was tired of the questions and the lies.

She sent a letter to Dr. Elmhurst.

Dear Dr. Elmhurst,

I needed to get away for a while. I will be in touch and will still appear for my scheduled office visits. Please don't worry.
Susan Kent

Sue arrived in Asheville and checked into the Grove Park Inn. She called the realtor and arranged to meet him in the morning. She also called B's manager and asked whom she should contact there.

She composed letters to both of her children explaining that she would be on extended leave due to her demanding work schedule. Her children should expect her to be traveling for at least six months.

It had been exactly one week since Sue's return from Hawaii. Mark and the kids would be looking for her now.

Chapter 27

Staying in school lessons the ravages of dementia.

Karen was worried. She had been calling her mother for two days and she had stopped by the house several times. The car was gone, but everything else looked pretty much the same.

She was going through her mother's closet when there was a knock on the door. She opened it.

"Is Sue here?" the man asked.

"No. Who are you?"

"I'm her fiancé. Who are you?"

"I'm her daughter," Karen answered in a stern voice.

The two looked at one another with shock.

"Fiancé?" she asked.

"Daughter?" Mark repeated.

"You'd better come in," Karen suggested.

"I don't understand. How could you be Sue's daughter? You're about the same age…and besides she doesn't have any kids."

"Oh, yes, she does. I have a younger brother, Kevin, and of course there's me."

"I still don't understand." Mark said, confused.

"Can I get you a beer or something? This is going to take a while." Karen asked.

"Do you have anything stronger? Like whiskey maybe?" Mark asked.

"Sure, be right back," Karen said.

Mark examined the pictures of Karen and Kevin on the bookshelf while Karen was gone.

"Here," she said as she handed Mark the glass. "I hope it's okay; I've never really made one before."

"It's fine, thank you," he said politely.

"I'll tell you everything I know," Karen started, "but it's still not going to explain everything."

Mark listened thoughtfully.

"My mother is 56 years old," she began. "A year or so ago, Mom began acting really kooky. She lost a lot of weight, became a much happier person, and started looking younger by the day. We don't know why or how. She's never explained anything to any of us. We don't know if she was taking drugs, having plastic surgery, or what."

"There's no way that Sue is 56; she doesn't even look 30. That's a totally crazy story. Why would you tell me this?" Mark asked.

"I know, that's what's so strange," Karen replied.

"This doesn't make any sense. This all sounds like some kind of weird made-up tale. Where is she?" Mark added.

"We don't know. She says she's on the road working for B's."

"I don't know what's going on here, what kind of game you are playing with me, but I don't like it…not any of it.

Do me a favor: tell Sue, whoever she is, that the engagement is off when you talk to her. I don't want any part of this," Mark said angrily.

"I'll do that. I'm sorry," Karen replied.

"Yeah, thanks," Mark said as he quickly departed.

Chapter 28

Soda ages people prematurely.

Sue drove to B's headquarters in the morning. She met with the head of marketing and the CEO. They discussed Sue's upcoming schedule and told her how thrilled they were that she was now living in Asheville.

Sue asked if it would be all right to color her hair. As long as it was a natural-looking color, the answer was affirmative.

She met with the realtor who took her to several residential neighborhoods.

"These are all too big for me," she said. "I need something that I can lock and go."

The realtor took her to several newly renovated apartment buildings in the downtown area. They were exactly what she was looking for. She chose a luxurious loft apartment and they started the paper work. If all went well, Sue would be able to move in on the first of the month.

She shook the realtor's hand and drove back to the Grove Park Inn, stopping at CVS to buy hair dye. She chose a deep red.

Sue ordered room service as she read the instructions for the dye. She noticed the dozens of messages on her phone. She ignored them all.

She put *Steel Magnolias* on the TV while she ate her Cobb salad and sipped on some wine. She perused the list of spa treatments at the hotel. She decided that a spa day was in order for the following day.

Sue went to bed early and hit the hotel gym first thing in the morning. Her perfect body looked even better in her tight black shorts and bright red halter-top.

Two very young men couldn't take their eyes off of her as she concentrated on her lunges and squats.

After her workout and some breakfast, she arrived at the spa for a full list of treatments. By the end of the day she was scrubbed, polished, massaged and had changed her long, now red hair to a shoulder length, edgy cut. She was completely relaxed and felt marvelous.

Taking advantage of her relaxed state, she decided to return some of her numerous phone calls. She started with Karen.

Karen's voice was cold, "Where are you, Mother?"

"I'm traveling. I told you I'd be gone," Sue said.

"No, Mother, you just disappeared," Karen answered.

"Karen, do we really need to do this? Can we just have a pleasant conversation?" Sue asked.

"I met your fiancé," Karen started.

"You what?" Sue asked, startled.

"You heard me," Karen repeated.

"What happened?" Sue's heart was pounding.

"He says to tell you that the engagement is off," Karen said flatly.

"Karen, what did you say to him?" Sue asked.

"The truth, as far as I know it," Karen said.

"Did you tell him who you are?" Sue asked.

"Yes," Karen replied.

Sue knew that she had been unmasked. There was no explaining her way out of this.

"I need to go now," she said as she hung up. She felt terrified. I really blew it, she thought. He was a good man, and I blew it!

So much for feeling relaxed. She wasn't up for any more calls at the moment.

Chapter 29

Only about 30% of the characteristics of aging are genetically determined. The other 70% are linked to lifestyle.

Sue pulled out her sexiest little black dress and highest heels. She slowly traced her lips with a red lipstick that matched the color of her newly polished nails and headed downstairs to the piano bar.

"A lemon drop, please," she said the bartender.

Within a moment, the seat next to her was occupied by one of the young men from the gym. He looked to be about 26 or 27.

"One for me too, please," he instructed the bartender.

"Cheers," he said, "to the most beautiful woman I've seen in a long time."

"Thank you," she said as she thought about whether or not to make up a fake story about herself.

"I'm Rick," he said, "and you are?"

"Marie, from Atlanta."

"Hello, Marie from Atlanta. It's nice to meet you. Would you like to dance?"

Sue took a swig of her drink and slid onto her feet. "That sounds wonderful!"

The two danced for an hour before returning to their drinks.

"Bartender, another round," Rick said.

"Grab your drink, then let's go outside for a little walk."

Sue picked up her drink and followed the attractive stranger outside.

Rick lit up a joint. "Here, want some?" he asked.

Sue had never tried marijuana before. Why not, she thought? She took the cigarette and inhaled slowly. It felt harsh on her lungs. She coughed hard. Immediately, she felt as if she were floating.

The couple returned to the dance floor. Everything was in slow motion. She felt wonderful, numb.

"Let's go to your room," Rick suggested.

Sue nodded. She felt as if she were in a dream and everything was good and happy.

"Do you have anything to drink?" Rick asked once inside the room.

"A full bar, over there," she pointed to the mini bar.

"Here," he said as he handed her a glass of vodka on the rocks. "We need to wake you up," he said as he reached into his pocket. He pulled out a small bag of cocaine.

Sue eyes grew large. She had never tried cocaine either. What the heck, she thought.

He poured a small amount onto the glass coffee table and divided into lines with his credit card. He took the first line.

"Here," he said, handing Sue the rolled up bill.

She took the bill from his hand and imitated the snorting sound that Rick had made. She pulled her head up quickly from the table.

"Wow!" she exclaimed, "That was fantastic!" Sue had an immediate rush from the drug.

Rick wasted no time in making his move. He leaned in towards Sue, pulling at the zipper on the back of her short, tight dress. She kissed him, feeling as if she were floating and flying all at the same time.

He quickly maneuvered Sue to the bed where he removed the remainder of her clothing. Rick spent a few moments in foreplay with his new partner, and then he lay her on the bed where he swiftly entered her.

Sex had never felt like this before! She felt as if she were floating in and out of her body. It was incredible!

When they were finished, Rick lit up another joint.

"Here, have some more, or you'll never be able to sleep," he said.

Sue took a long toke and floated off to sleep.

When she awakened in the morning, Rick was gone, and the drugs had worn off. She felt a deep pang in the pit of her stomach as she recalled her conversation with Karen.

Chapter 30

The average life expectancy by the year 2040 will be 86 for men and 91.5 for women.

Sue maintained a low profile at the hotel for a few days. She didn't want to run into Rick and she was embarrassed by her behavior. She was also still reeling from the reality of losing Mark.

She mailed the ring back to Mark, certified mail, and no note. There was nothing to say. She'd been caught in her lies and there would be no way to explain.

She drove to High Point to window shop for furniture ideas for her new apartment. She wouldn't need much.

At last, Sue decided that it was time to face the music and return the rest of her calls. First, she called Karen again.

"How are you?" Sue asked her daughter.

"I'm okay, Mom, confused, hurt, angry. I really feel that I've lost my mother."

Sue sighed, "I'm sorry, Honey. I didn't expect things to turn out this way. I promise to call you once a week, okay?"

"Okay, Mom, I miss you," she said sadly.

"I miss you too."

Sue sighed again. That call had gone better than expected. Next she called Kevin.

"Hi, how are you, Honey?" she asked.

"I miss you, Mom. Are you okay?"

"Yes, just working. I promise to do a better job of staying in touch."

"I worry about you, Mom. Please let me know if you need anything. I love you."

"I love you, too."

She tried to reach Margie. She left a message.

Her last call was to John.

"I've been going out of my mind with worry, Sue. When are you coming back? I'm waiting for you."

"I'm fine, John. Please don't wait for me. There is no more 'us' anymore."

"I'll never give up, Sue. I love you so much."

"Okay, John. I just wanted to let you know that I'm all right."

She was exhausted. She needed to let off some steam. She had really enjoyed dancing the other night, but she couldn't afford to run into Rick. She called the concierge.

"Can you recommend a place in town to go dancing?" she asked.

The concierge gave her a few choices.

She dressed in a royal blue short jumpsuit, bright red heels and the same bright, red lipstick.

She took a cab to Roxie's. The music was loud and the lights dim. She made her way through the dense crowd to the bar.

"Cosmo, please," she said to the bartender.

She looked around the room trying to make out the wide array of faces.

"Don't you just love the way a Cosmo goes down so smoothly?" the exotic looking woman standing next to her at the bar asked.

"Yes, they're very smooth," Sue eyed the woman closely.

The lanky brunette closed her heavily decorated eyes and swayed to the music, seeming to get lost in it.

Sue took a sip of her drink and continued to watch the woman out of the corner of her eye.

The woman touched Sue's hair playfully. "It's sooo soft," she said with a sultry voice.

Sue stiffened, feeling uncomfortable with the stranger's touch.

The woman ran her hand lightly and down the length of Sue's arm. Sue froze.

"Come dance with me," the woman urged.

'But, I…," Sue stammered.

Before she had an opportunity to object, the woman had grabbed her by the hand and they were on the middle of the dance floor. The woman swayed gently to the music. Sue stood, frozen. She had never danced with a woman before!

The woman ignored Sue's objections, and placed her hand on Sue's hips, urging her, without words, to follow her lead. Sue tried to follow, but felt embarrassed by the situation. She watched intently as the woman completely let herself go with the music.

Sue was relieved when the song ended. "Let's go back to the bar," Sue insisted.

The woman shrugged and followed Sue back to the bar. Sue immediately took a large sip of her Cosmopolitan. The sultry woman intrigued her.

"What's your name?" Sue asked.

"So-fi-a," she responded slowly.

"I'm Sue," she added, "You're accent is unique. Where are you from?"

"Brazil."

"Do you want to feel incredible, Sue? Ever had one of these?" She placed a white capsule on the bar next to Sue's drink.

Sue shook her head. "What is it?" she asked.

"Molly. Try it with me. You will never feel so amazing in your whole life."

"Where's yours?" Sue asked.

"I already took one, but I'll take another with you."

Sofia pulled a second pill out of her tiny purse.

"Cheers," she said.

The two women swallowed their pills at the same time, washing them down with their sweet cocktails.

Chapter 31

On average, an elderly person makes about $30,000 per year.

The two women ordered a second Cosmo, took a few sips and headed back to the dance floor. Sue found herself becoming less self-conscious and more in tune with the music.

A half hour passed on the dance floor. Sofia took both of Sue's hands in hers. Sue felt as if she were floating…closer and closer to Sofia. Sofia pulled Sue close and allowed her hands to gently caress Sue's body.

Sue closed her eyes to experience the full sensation of Sofia's touch. Sofia stroked Sue's hair and tenderly kissed her on the lips. It felt amazing to Sue.

"Come," Sofia instructed. "Come with me."

Without uttering a word, Sue followed her new friend out of the club. Moments later, they were standing at the door of Sofia's loft apartment.

Sofia opened the door with her key and pulled Sue inside. The apartment was sparsely decorated with a few simple pieces of furniture, several large oil paintings and hardwood floors with various faux animal furs and pillows thrown about.

Sofia put on some jazz and dimmed the lights. Then she led Sue to the edge of her queen size bed.

Sue stood motionless as Sofia removed her own dress with a single pull of a tie on the back of her neck.

Sue found herself staring at one of the most beautiful bodies she had ever seen. Sofia was tall, with dark olive skin, smoldering dark eyes, and luxurious dark brown hair to the middle of her back. Her body was lean and muscular.

Seemingly unable to move or speak, Sue stood motionless as Sofia lovingly moved her hands over Sue's arms, back and neck. Methodically, she removed Sue's clothing, item by item. Sue was overcome with a tingling sensation, as if every cell of her body were on high alert.

Sofia grabbed Sue behind her neck and pulled her close for a long, open-mouthed kiss. Sue could feel the passionate pressure on every part of Sofia's tongue touching hers.

Sofia pulled her to the white fur that topped her bed. Sue felt as though she would explode with joy. The feel of the soft fur combined with Sofia's sensual touch was almost too much to bear.

The Brazilian deliberately kissed Sue from her mouth to her breasts. It was the most marvelous sensation she had ever experienced!

Sofia traced Sue's labia with her tongue. Sue grabbed the fur beneath her fingers and arched her back. Sofia went deeper with her tongue, sequentially, in a circular motion.

She teased Sue by varying her intensity until she exploded in ecstasy.

Sue absorbed every element of her atmosphere. She felt Sofia's touch on her skin and hair, the rhythmical spinning of the fan overhead and the faint stirring of air that it invoked, the distant sound of jazz still playing in the background and the delicious aroma of Sofia's tanned skin.

The two women held one another, stroking each other's bodies and intently looking into one another's eyes.

Sue had not uttered a word since she had stepped into Sofia's apartment. The two drifted off into a dreamy state of sleep.

Chapter 32

Facial exercises will not prevent wrinkles.

Sue opened her eyes. The small apartment was flooded with light and the aroma of coffee was pungent. She turned her head to see Sofia, dressing in a purple silk kimono, pouring coffee and humming quietly to the faint Reggae music in the background.

Without turning around, Sofia asked, "Coffee?"

Startled by the offer, Sue replied quickly, "Yes, please."

This was an awkward situation for Sue. She had never waked up in a woman's bed before. How did this work?

Sofia placed a small cup of hot coffee on the bedside table.

Sue studied the woman's face. She looked much different in the light of day, without all of the makeup and without the drug.

Sofia was more exotic than beautiful. She had a large space between the teeth in the center of her wide, white smile.

"The shower is in there if you're so inclined," she said as she pointed down the hall.

Sofia was acting so casual about all of this. Sue declined the offer for a shower.

"I need to get going," she said awkwardly. "It was a fun evening." She didn't know what else to say.

"Fun? Yes. We'll have to do it again sometime." She kissed Sue on the lips.

"Okay, then. See you later." Sue scooted out the door in a hurry.

Sue returned to her hotel room and plopped herself on the large sofa. She replayed the events of the night before in her head.

What have I done, she wondered? She had never felt attracted to a woman before. She questioned her sexuality. She questioned everything!

Suddenly, she felt all alone. She called her kids and tried Margie, once again. The kids were fine and Margie still wasn't answering the phone.

She checked her email. There was an itinerary from B's. Starting on Monday she would be booked every day for the following two weeks.

With a couple of days of freedom left, she chose to go shopping.

The concierge recommended a few places. She headed to the downtown area and bought numerous pairs of shoes.

Then she walked a few blocks up the street to a small boutique and purchased a new wardrobe of cocktail dresses, cashmere sweaters, dress pants, and some pearl jewelry as well as some classic basics for her wardrobe.

Chapter 33

Eating large quantities of oily fish will not prevent skin from aging.

Sue's schedule was hectic. Catalogue work required long hours in the studio.

She was exhausted by the end of each day and was happy to relax in her hotel room and order room service.

She couldn't get Sofia out of her mind. She thought about her constantly. She wanted to see her again, but was afraid.

She managed to get through the two weeks of work and was given a week off before the next assignment.

The apartment was ready. Sue spent an entire afternoon ordering furniture that she had seen in High Point. She was happy with her new environment. The apartment was all hers without history of her kids, or John.

Sofia was still very much on her mind. She had to see her. Sue dressed provocatively in a low-cut mini dress and her highest heels. She arrived at Roxie's and headed straight to the bar.

"Cosmo, please," she requested.

She searched the room for Sofia's familiar face. Sipping the drink, she waited and watched.

Finally, she asked the bartender, "Have you seen Sofia around?"

"The Brazilian?" he asked.

"Yes, that's the one."

"Sure, she's always in and out. Haven't seen her tonight though."

"Okay. Thank you." Now what, she wondered.

She walked to Sofia's apartment. Her heart was pounding as she knocked on the door. She could hear music inside. Sofia answered the door. "Ola, Beautiful! Where have you been?"

"May I come in?" Sue asked, embarrassed.

Sofia opened the door wider. Sue stepped inside and was startled to see a woman there.

"Oh, I'm sorry," Sue started.

"Sorry, why? Please stay. This is Ju-li-a," she said with her heavy accent. "She can be your friend too."

Sue nodded at the woman shyly.

"Would you like to have a drink?" Julia asked.

She was a fairly attractive woman with bright red hair, a nose ring and numerous tattoos.

"Yes, please." Sue answered.

"Here, have some of this first," she handed Sue a pipe.

"What is it?" she asked.

"Opium. You will feel wonderful!" she added.

Anything to take the edge off, Sue thought.

She took a long inhale and immediately felt a warm sensation from her head to her toes.

The three women sat on the faux fur throw rug in the middle of Sophia's open living room. They chatted, sipped their drinks and passed the pipe around.

Sophia opened her hand towards Sue. She held three white capsules in the palm of her hand. Sue accepted the offer. The three each swallowed their pill at the same time. Sue was already soaring.

Sue watched as her two companions started kissing one another. She was overcome with jealousy. Sofia switched her attention from Julia to Sue, stroking her hair and kissing her. Sue felt a shiver run through her entire body as Sofia touched her.

Sue ignored Julia and focused on the touch and smell of Sofia. She was intoxicating. Julia undressed as she watched the women embrace, then she approached the women, joining the interaction.

Sue stiffened as Julia touched her. Sofia and Julia joined together and removed Sue's dress and underwear. Sofia quickly slipped out of her sarong.

Sue was overcome by the sensation of two women touching and fondling her on the fleecy fur rug. She lost track of who was doing what to her; she just knew that the she was in ecstasy.

She was lost in a sea of hands, fingers and mouths. The orgy seemingly continued for hours. Sue wanted to please Sofia just as Sofia had pleased her. She did not know what to do other than to mimic what Sofia had done to her.

Sue slowly approached the patch of pink, tender skin in front of her, not knowing what to expect. She was immediately surprised by Sofia's wetness. Sue gently rolled her tongue around Sofia's vulva and was struck by the intense rose color of her lover's labia as her excitement heightened. Sue became more aggressive with her tongue as she realized how much pleasure Sofia was experiencing. Sue felt satisfaction as she found that she was able to control the intensity of her beloved's enjoyment.

The more pleasure that Sofia experienced, the more excited Sue became. As Sofia grabbed Sue's shoulders and dug her fingers into Sue's flesh, Sue became more adventuresome, experimenting with the motion and depth of her tongue. As Sofia's enjoyment increased, Sue's passion heightened, as it never had before. Sue was singly focused on her lover's satisfaction, so much so that she had completely forgotten Julia's presence.

Eventually, the three women fell asleep entangled in one another's arms, legs and bodies.

Sue awakened a few hours later. She looked at the two women sleeping beside her and felt mortified. She quickly put on her underwear, clothes and shoes and darted out the door.

Chapter 34

Anti-aging creams containing marine algae or caviar eggs
are not effective skin rejuvenators.

Sue was in a full panic. Now she had slept with two
women! She was so confused by her feelings for Sofia that
she cried for two hours. It was the first time she had cried
since starting on the product.

She didn't leave her apartment for days. She called
everyone she could think of; family, old friends.
Connecting with her past had suddenly become very
important, but Sofia was continuously on her mind.

Sue threw herself into her work, hoping that exhaustion
would chase Sofia from her thoughts.

Her scheduled appointment with Dr. Elmhurst was
approaching and she promised him that she would be
there. She planned a quick round trip to Reno. She had no
intention of seeing anyone she knew while she was there.

When she arrived at the clinic, Dr. Elmhurst greeted her enthusiastically, "Sue! I've been concerned about you. How are you? You look fantastic!" he said.

"I'm okay, Doctor. I just needed a change of scenery for a while."

"How's that going for you?" he asked.

"Well, it's interesting, to say the least." Sue commented.

"Care to elaborate?" The doctor asked.

"Not really, though I would like to see Shelby while I'm here, if that's possible."

"Of course, it is. Now, let's get down to the business at hand. We're going to run all the tests today. You're going to be here for quite some time."

"That's not a problem, Doctor. I have nowhere to be at the moment."

"Good! Then let's begin," Dr. Elmhurst said.

After four hours of testing, Sue was free to see Shelby.

"So, what's going on, Sue? What's been happening in your life? I heard that had you moved away."

"Everything in my life has changed. I was living such a lie here. I just had to get far enough away to think things through. Now, I honestly don't know what's going on. I think that I'm in love."

"Really? That's great! Tell me about it," Shelby said.

"I don't know how to explain it. I've never felt this way before and the relationship is brand new. We don't know very much about one another."

"I really need to speak to you more often, Shelby. So much has happened I wouldn't know where to begin."

"You seemed unusually stressed today, Sue. What's going on?"

"I'm overwhelmed with conflicting feelings and emotions. I don't know who I am any more. I used to think I knew exactly who I was, but know I question everything, even the most basic elements of myself as a person," Sue said.

"That sounds like a lot to deal with, Sue. Tell me more so I can try and help you," Shelby suggested.

Sue sighed heavily, "I'm not sure that I can even put what I'm feeling into words. I'm just overwhelmed, plain and simple," Sue said.

"How can I help you with this, Sue?" Shelby asked.

"I don't have any idea," Sue answered honestly.

"Well, how are things with your kids, work, your ex?" Shelby asked.

"Things are actually better with the kids these days. We talk more often. I think it helps that they can't see me…what I look like."

"The job is great. I travel quite a bit, work long hours, but I enjoy it. I don't talk to John at all, but I don't think that he's given up."

Sue debated about whether or not she should tell Shelby about Sofia, Julia and the drugs. She decided not to broach the subject at this point.

"You're welcome to see me anytime, Sue, but the appointments have to be in person."

"I understand. Thank you, Shelby."

Sue filled out her form before leaving.

Sue checked into the Grand Sierra Resort, feeling emotionally spent, ordered room service and hoped that no one would see her before her early morning flight back to Asheville. It felt strange to her to be in her hometown and not see her family, friends, or even her house. She felt sad and weary as she dozed off to sleep.

Chapter 35

Some anti-aging superfoods include olive oil, blueberries, fish, nuts red wine and yogurt.

Sue had one thing on her mind as she headed east across the country: she had to see Sofia again and as soon as possible.

She did her best to look her sexiest, wearing a revealing red dress with the back cut out to the top of her buttocks. Sue tried to appear casual as she entered the bar at Roxie's.

"Lemon drop," she instructed the bartender. She slowly sipped her cocktail as she scrutinized the room for Sofia's familiar face. Her heart was pounding. It pounded even harder once she locked in on the radiant smile of her lover.

Sofia was sitting at a small table with several women; she was obviously flirting with one of them. Sue took a deep breath, picked up her drink and walked slowly toward the table. There she stood, silently waiting for Sofia to notice her.

Sofia rubbed the leg of the woman sitting next to her as she looked up to see Sue standing there.

Sofia smiled, "Well…look what the cat dragged in. It's my little disappearing friend. How are you, Querida?" she asked as she lightly ran her hand up and down Sue's arm.

Sue's heart melted when Sofia called her by that name. "I'm fine. I've been away."

"Well, come sit with us," Sofia instructed.

Sue studied the faces of the women at the table. They seemed unfriendly as they ignored her. She took a seat next to Sofia.

"For you, my Querida," Sofia said as she opened her hand to Sue, revealing a small, white capsule in her hand.

Sue took the pill without hesitation. She wanted to feel good and forget the awkwardness of the moment.

"Come," Sofia commanded. "Dance with me."

Sue followed her to the floor and was instantly lost in the loud music. She could feel the drug kicking in. Sue's mind was focused on her partner and how wonderful she felt and how she smelled of flowers and citrus. Sue closed her eyes and erased the image of the people in the club. She had Sofia in her arms and she was happy.

The two returned to the table and ordered another drink.

"Let's everyone come to my place. It's time for a private party, no?"

The women all raised their glasses in agreement.

Sue felt panicked. She wanted to be alone with Sofia.

"Are you coming, Querida?" She asked Sue as she held the hand of the woman next to her.

Sue swallowed hard and nodded. Anything to be with the one that she loved.

Sue felt a pang of jealousy as she walked behind Sofia and her friend holding hands.

One of the women went to work making drinks, another picked out some music and a third lit up a pipe. It had the familiar aroma of opium.

Moments later Sue felt lost in a sea of bodies. She was unable to lift the fog from her head and she felt panicky as she was unable to distinguish one body from another.

Suddenly she felt nauseous. She ran into the bathroom and vomited. Then she passed out on the cold tile floor.

Chapter 36

Going to bed with makeup on can age your skin up to 7 times faster than if your face is clean.

Sue came back into consciousness about an hour later. She splashed some cold water on her face and stepped quietly into the living room. The four remaining women were still heavily involved in their passionate heap on the floor.

Sue watched motionless as another woman made love to her lover. It made her feel sick all over again. She quickly covered her mouth with her hand and ran out the front door.

Still in a haze, Sue hailed a cab back to her small apartment. She crawled into her new, four-poster bed and cried herself to sleep.

She awakened in the morning feeling refreshed, as usual, but she couldn't get the image of Sofia with another woman out of her mind. She did her best to distract herself by heading to the gym. After an hour, and drenched in sweat, Sofia was still on her mind. She had to see her alone, to talk to her.

Showered and changed, Sue gathered her nerve and headed to Sofia's apartment late in the afternoon.

Sofia answered the door in her purple silk kimono.

"Querida! Where did you go last night? You just disappeared!"

"I wasn't feeling well. Can we talk?" Sue asked nervously.

"Surely, Beautiful, please come in." Sofia invited her inside.

"By the way, Sofia, what does 'Querida' mean?" Sue asked.

"Desired one."

Sue's heart melted once again until she looked around and saw one of the women from the night before sitting on Sofia's tiny deck, drinking coffee.

"Can we talk, alone?"

Sofia gave her a look of disapproval. "If it's so important, okay," she said, motioning for the other woman to leave.

"Now, what is so important, Querida? Would you like some coffee?"

"Yes, please," Sue answered.

The two women sat in Sofia's open living room.

"I want to be with you," Sue started.

"I want to be with you too," Sofia said while twirling a piece of Sue's hair.

"No, I want to be with you, alone. No one else."

Sofia removed her hand from Sue's hair. "Ah, Querida, but that's not me. My life is all about big love, love with as many as possible, sharing with everyone, feeling good. I'm sorry, Beautiful, but what you want cannot ever be."

Sue felt the tears welling up in her eyes. She grabbed her purse and without another word, ran out the door before Sofia could see her crying. She ran down the small staircase and quickly unlocked her Lexus parked outside. She was crying so hard that she could hardly see to make the short drive back to her apartment.

For the next week, she didn't eat, barely slept, and didn't go out of her apartment. She lost seven pounds. This was the worst feeling she had ever experienced in her life.

Chapter 37

The number of people aged 80 and older will quadruple in the period 2000 to 2050.

Sue showed up to work bright and early Monday morning. She checked in with her boss.

"My God, Sue, are you all right? You're so thin!"

"I'm fine," she said, trying to hold back the tears. It's been a rough week."

"You need to put a little weight back on or we're not going to be able to use you anymore."

"I will. I'm sorry."

"Well, here's your itinerary for the week. You and the crew are headed down to Hilton Head for the week. Lots of beach shots. Have fun!"

Sue was relieved to be getting out of town. The beach sounded perfect to her.

She arrived at the hotel in a van with her wardrobe, a cameraman, a hair and makeup person and a lighting expert…all men.

Sue checked into her room and took in the panoramic view of the Atlantic. It was her first time in Hilton Head.

She had arranged to meet "the guys" downstairs in the bar in an hour.

The three men were sitting at the bar, drinking beer, when she walked in.

"What will you have?" one of them asked Sue.

"I'll have what you're having," she said.

They chatted casually for a while and ordered another beer, then the photographer placed something into Sue's palm. "Take it to the bathroom," he instructed her.

Sue excused herself and headed to the ladies room. Once inside the stall, she opened the small, folded piece of paper and carefully searched it's contents. It was cocaine, just as she had expected. She took out one of her keys and scooped a small amount onto the end of the key. Forcefully she sniffed the powder, and then repeated the same process on the other nostril.   Feeling invigorated, she returned to the bar and thanked the photographer for the boost.

The group made a decision to find a livelier place to drink, so they congregated at the Montego Bay. The place was packed and the music loud.

Before they could order a drink, a man asked Sue to dance. She danced for hours, stopping occasionally to order a drink.

The crew interrupted Sue on the dance floor saying that they were going to bed and would see her bright and early the next morning for a photo shoot on the beach.

"Are you sure you're all right?" one of them asked, looking at her dance partner.

"Yes, I'm fine. See you in the morning." Sue answered.

Sue resumed dancing.

"Let's get out of here," her young partner suggested.

They walked back toward Sue's hotel, stopping at the pool. While sharing a lounge chair, the young man pulled a small glass container out of his pants pocket. Attached to the top of the container was a small spoon. He scooped some white powder onto the spoon and handed it to Sue. She sniffed forcefully and repeated on the other side after he reloaded the spoon. He then took two hits for himself.

"Skinny dip?" he asked.

Sue looked around at the empty pool area. She smiled. "Sure."

Within seconds they were naked and quietly splashing and carousing in the pool. The man grabbed her and pulled her playfully through the cold water in a circular motion. Sue giggled with glee."

"Let's go to your room," he said.

They grabbed their clothes and swiftly pulled them on over their wet bodies. Their clothes came off once again as soon as they were inside the room.

Sue took control of the situation, pushing the man onto her bed and placing herself on top of him.

She felt nothing like she had when she was with Sofia. With Sofia her senses had been heightened and at the same time she had felt relaxed and open. Now, her senses were heightened, but she had felt like a cat ready to pounce. She was able to continue encounter with the young stranger for hours.

It was four o'clock before she was able to go to sleep and she had a nine A.M. call for makeup and hair. When the alarm went off, she nudged her partner to get out of bed. It was time for him to leave. She looked in the mirror and to her amazement, she looked beautiful and rested even after only four hours of sleep.

The workday went well. They shot on the beach for a full eight hours before calling it a day and the crew made plans to meet in the same hotel bar again.

The rest of the week went the same way. They would meet in the bar, drink, do a few lines of coke, and then move to another bar. Sue would pick up someone new and take him back to her room. Then she would get up, go to work and do the same thing all over again.

Chapter 38

In the United States, women outlive men by average of
five years.

Sue was disappointed to return to Asheville. The beach
had been a nice distraction for her from thinking about
Sofia. She felt an ache every time she thought of her.

Sue called the cameraman from the Hilton Head shoot.
"Meet me for a drink?" she asked.

"Sure, there's a great band playing at Lucky Luke's
tonight. See you there at nine."

Sue was feeling frisky so she dressed accordingly in a
playful leopard print mini dress and a pair of well-worn
cowboy boots. She made her hair look messy and used
more dark eye makeup than usual. She put on a pair of
huge bronze, dangly earrings and was ready to go.

Her friend was waiting at the bar in the large venue when she arrived. The music was fantastic and the place was jammed.

"Beer?" he asked. Sue nodded.

"So, what's up?" he asked, looking curious.

"I was just wondering if you could hook me up?"

"With the little friend in my pocket?" he asked. Sue nodded.

"How much?" he asked. She shrugged.

"An eight ball?" he asked. Sue nodded. She had no idea what he was talking about.

"Meet me for coffee tomorrow and I'll set you up. In the meantime I slipped a little something into your purse to tide you over into your purse. The side pocket."

Sue smiled and kissed her friend on the cheek. "You're a doll," she said.

Sue returned from the ladies' room feeling on top of the world.

"Will you be all right if I leave you here?" he asked.

Sue looked around. "Sure," she said, "I'll be fine."

It didn't take long for a man in his early twenties to ask Sue to dance. She accepted.

The two danced until closing time, then walked the short distance to Sue's apartment. They did a couple of lines and a two more cocktails before falling into bed and making love.

Sue slept in before making a feigned effort to work out at the gym. She did a little cardio and a few weights before calling it a day.

Once home, she called her kids to see how they were doing. She missed them more than she had ever expected. They were now talking three times a week and their relationships were improving.

"How are you, Honey?" Sue asked Karen.

"Mom, are you sitting down?"

"Yes, why?" Sue asked.

"I'm engaged, Mom. Gary asked me last night."

"Congratulations, Honey! When is the wedding?"

"I don't know yet, Mom, but I want you to be here to help me plan everything. I miss you so much."

"We probably won't get married until next year. That will give us plenty of time. You'll be home soon, won't you, Mom? You said six months."

Sue held back the tears, "I'm so happy for you, Karen. I'm so proud of you. Of course, I want to help you plan everything."

"Thanks, Mom. I miss you."

"I miss you too."

Sue hung up the phone and wept. Now what was she going to do? She couldn't show up to own daughter's wedding looking ten years younger than the bride!

She pulled out the small baggie and dumped some white powder onto her coffee table. She took two hits and thought about her predicament.

There was only one thing to do: go back to the Lucky Luke's!

Chapter 39

The youngest Pope was 11 years old.

Sue was feeling morose, so she dressed all in black, with thick, heavy eyeliner. She loaded her thick, short hair with gel, giving it a piecy, edgy look.

A country band was playing at the Lucky Luke's. Sue ordered a lemon drop and the bartender carded her. She was the only person she knew of who had a fake ID making herself younger than she actually was! No one would ever believe that her 57th birthday was right around the corner! The crowd was a bit thinner than the night before.

Her young friend, Randy, appeared and he was all smiles. She hadn't really noticed before how adorable he actually was.

He couldn't have been more than 23 or 24, with light brown hair and sparkling, clear blue eyes. He was about

5'10", athletic and spoke with the local Southern drawl. He was clearly happy to see Sue.

"Can I buy you a drink?" he asked her.

"Sure, have a seat," she offered. "Would you like a bump?" she asked.

"Yeah, thanks," he answered.

Sue slid the small vial into his hand. When Randy returned from the bathroom, the two hit the dance floor. Sue was happy for the moment, not thinking about Sofia or Karen's wedding.

"The music is a little slow. Let's go to your place," Randy suggested.

They walked hand in hand the short distance to Sue's small apartment.

"I have something for us to try," he said as he pulled a small piece of foil from his pocket.

"What is it?" Sue asked not recognizing it's contents.

"Hashish," he responded.

"Really? I've never tried it," she said matter of factly.

"It's very mellow. You'll like it," he said.

Sue put on some soft music and poured two glasses of Grey Goose on the rocks. She inhaled the thick smoke and immediately felt tranquil.

"It's a little like opium," she commented as she exhaled the thick smoke.

"Yeah, kind of, I guess," Randy responded.

The two sat quietly enjoying the serene high.

Eventually, they made their way to Sue's bed. Everything felt like it was in slow motion. Sue enjoyed exploring her young lover's body with her hands and tongue. Randy held her closely as they dozed off to sleep.

Chapter 40

After the age of 30, the brain shrinks a quarter of a percent
in mass each year.

Sue had a busy schedule at work. She was traveling a lot
and relying on cocaine every day to keep herself going.

She talked to Karen almost every day, making plans for
the wedding. She was lonely, having no friends of her
own. Randy was the only person in her life. He was kind
and smart, but hardly a suitable match for a 57-year-old
woman. She enjoyed his company, but still yearned to be
with Sofia.

After months of leaving messages with Margie, her
persistence finally paid off. Margie called her.

"This is a surprise," Sue said as she answered the phone.

"I've been talking to Karen and she's been filling me in.
I'm glad that you two are talking again," Margie started.

"Me too," Sue said.

"So, I hear that you've been working hard. Are you coming home soon to help plan the wedding?" Margie asked.

"I hope so. Tell me, what's been going on with you?" Sue asked.

Sue listened, feeling like a complete outsider, as Margie described the day-to-day details that used to be part of Sue's life. She felt sad, like she would never be part of that life again.

The two women chatted for an hour and the phone conversations became a regular part of their day from that time on. Sue felt happy to have both Karen and Margie back in her life.

The next few months were busy with work and partying with Randy at night. Together, they experimented with various drugs. Sue enjoyed cocaine during the day, but also enjoyed the euphoric feelings that came from MDMA, marijuana, hashish and opium. The couple enjoyed experimenting by trying two drugs together at the same time.

Their lovemaking was always different, depending on which drug they were taking at the time. Sue still liked Molly the best for sex, especially when adding a little opium to the mix.

Chapter 41

The oldest animal in the world is "Ming", the 405-year-old clam, discovered in 2007.

It was time for Sue's scheduled visit to see Dr. Elmhurst. This time she wanted to be especially careful not to run into anyone that she knew while she was in Reno.

She wore an ash blond wig and checked into the Grand Sierra Resort. She took a cab the short distance to the doctor's office on Mill St.

"You look so different, Sue," he commented.

"It's a wig," she responded.

"You look to be about 20 now, and I'm guessing that our test results are going to back that up. How are you feeling?"

Sue decided to be honest with the doctor.

"Considering that I haven't been taking care of myself, I feel pretty good."

Dr. Elmhurst looked concerned. "What do you mean that you're not taking care of yourself?"

"I haven't been going to they gym much and I've been experimenting with drugs." Sue figured he would know from her blood tests.

He looked at Sue over the top of his glasses. "I can't condone what you are doing, but I need to explain something to you. The product enables your body to replenish your cells each and every day. In other words, you wake up every morning with fresh, clean cells. In essence, there are no repercussions from your drug use."

"Are you kidding?" she asked, astonished.

"It's true," he said firmly.

"That explains a lot. I wake up every morning, looking and feeling good, no matter what I've done the night before."

"There is one thing, though," the doctor continued, "It concerns me why you are taking drugs. I think you need to talk to Shelby about this. I'm scheduling an extended appointment for you with her when we're finished here."

"Thank you, Doctor."

"Now, let's take a look at your latest test results. We're over two years into the trial an you are now the equivalent of a twenty year old."

"What happens now, Dr. Elmhurst? Am I going to become an embryo?"

Dr. Elmhurst chuckled, "Of course not. You are at your peak and you're going to stay this age as long as you continue to take the product."

"What if I want to adjust my age, and cut back on the dosage?"

"We've tried that and it doesn't seem to work. It's either your real biological age or twenty. You will be able to live to the equivalent of 125 years of age, though you will continue to look like you're twenty."

"Will the product be on the market soon? Will I ever be able to talk about this or share my experiences with others going through the same thing?"

"We don't know the answer to those questions yet. You committed to three years, Sue. We'll discuss what happens after that when your trial is finished."

"Okay, Doctor. This hasn't been easy, you know."

"I do know, Sue. You've been the perfect candidate, but I want you to start taking care of yourself." Dr. Elmhurst shook Sue's hand.

Chapter 42

After the age of 30, the brain begins to lose about 50,000 neurons per day.

Shelby was waiting for Sue after her appointment.

"How are you, Sue? Cute wig!" Shelby commented.

"Thank you. I'm incognito today," Sue remarked.

"Well, step into my office and tell me all about it."

"Is it okay if I start at the beginning since we have extra time?" Sue asked.

"Yes, please do," Shelby said.

"It all started before I left town. Everything was falling apart. The lies were catching up with me. I had to get away, to think, to breathe."

"I moved to North Carolina for work. It didn't take long before I started experimenting with drugs. They immediately made me forget my pain and confusion. I could just be in the moment when I was high."

"Then I met a woman and I fell in love with her. When she rejected me, I went off the deep end and haven't recovered since."

"I didn't realize that you're gay," Shelby interjected.

"Neither did I. Sofia was intoxicating, one of a kind."

"So, tell me what's been going on since then?" Shelby inquired.

"For a while, I was with a different guy every night. I've been using coke every day, but experimenting with all kinds of different drugs at night."

"How has that been working for you?" Shelby asked.

"I've been having lots of fun, I guess. I'm with one guy now. He's sweet, but it's not love or anything. After all, he's young enough to be my son."

"I would suggest to you, Sue, that you are not homosexual. Did you ever consider that perhaps the young woman and the drugs were just distractions from everything in your life that is bothering you and hurting?"

"No, I never thought of it that way. I just feel that my world is closing in on me. My daughter is getting married and I want to be there for her, but how can I? I now look years younger than she does. The drugs help me to forget all of the lies for the moment."

"What do you want, Sue? Do you want to be 20 and have the perfect body that you have now, or would you rather go back to the old, fat Sue and still have your family? It's entirely up to you."

"I don't know, Shelby. I live in hell, half in one life, and half in another, fitting in nowhere."

"I'd like for you to stop using the recreational drugs, and I would like for you to consider why you are using them. You need to have a clear mind to make these important decisions."

"I will try my best to do that. Thank you, Shelby." Sue had no intention of stopping her drug use.

"Remember to fill out the questionnaire before you leave, Sue."

"Okay, see you next time, Shelby."

Shelby shook her hand.

Chapter 43

At age 25, we have 6% bone mineral. At age 70, we have 5% bone mineral.

Sue returned to work Monday morning. She was scheduled to have a busy month of travel. Her photographer friend was keeping her supplied with cocaine, and she was using it every day.

She and Randy would meet at night, party for awhile, and head back to her place for more cocaine and whatever drug Randy would bring along. They smoked opium; marijuana, hashish and they even tried LSD.

Sue would awaken early every morning feeling rejuvenated and refreshed. She would show up to work on time and work professionally, even though she was wired on cocaine most of the time.

Sue and Randy took weekend trips on his motorcycle to nearby Lake Lure, Lake James, and the Blue Ridge

Parkway. Occasionally, they camped, bringing along their varied drug supply.

One Saturday night, the couple had been out partying at the clubs. They were feeling especially festive that night. Sue dressed in one of her new cocktail dresses and some simple, sparkly heels and they headed out for a night of dancing. They did a little coke before they left her apartment, and more when they returned home.

"I have a surprise for you," Randy said as he pulled a small piece of foil from his pocket. He opened the foil revealing the small black object inside.

"What is it?" Sue asked inquisitively.

"Heroin, black tar," he said smiling.

Sue froze. "Heroin? I don't think that's a good idea," she said.

"Oh come on, Sue. We're going to smoke it, not shoot it. It's perfectly safe. I hear it's a high like no other. It will mellow us out after all that coke tonight."

Sue remembered what Dr. Elmhurst had told her, that basically there were no repercussions from her drug use.

"Okay," she agreed reluctantly.

Randy pulled out a small pipe and placed a small piece of the black material inside. He pulled out a lighter and carefully lit the pipe. He took a long drag and slowly exhaled the white smoke.

"Awesome," he said as he handed the pipe to Sue.

Cautiously, she took the pipe from Randy as he lit it for her. She took a big draw and held the smoke in her lungs for a moment before letting it go. She was floating. It was the most euphoric experience of her life. She smiled at her partner, he grinned back.

The two sat motionless for hours listening to the soft indie rock in the background and occasionally taking a toke on the pipe. Eventually, they crawled into bed, watching the slow ceiling fan whirl overhead.

Chapter 44

The ashes of a cremated person average about nine pounds.

Sue awakened as the sun shone through her large bedroom window. She stretched, feeling revived and rested. Then she turned to Randy and gave him a nudge. There was no reaction.

She whispered in his ear, "Time to get up sleepy head!"

There was still no movement. Sue shoved him hard. Her heart was pounding. She turned him on his back, his eyes were open but he wasn't breathing. She quickly checked for a pulse. He was dead! Oh my God, Randy is dead! What was she going to do?

She needed to call an ambulance right away, but first she had to destroy any evidence. She quickly grabbed her purse and pulled out a large vial of cocaine, then looked at the coffee table for any drug paraphernalia. She snatched the pipe, foil and lighter and quickly wiped the table with a paper towel and some Windex.

Now what? She had no friends in town, no one to call. She flushed the cocaine and the heroin down the toilet. She took the glass vial and foil, put it in a baggie and taped the baggie to the underside of her small deck. Then she suddenly remembered the bottle of little red pills. How would she explain those to the police? She added the bottle to the bag and retaped it to the under side of the deck.

She checked Randy's body for any sign of evidence. She wiped his nose with a damp rag, and then she headed to the bathroom to splash some cold water on her face.

She called 911.

"What's your emergency?" the women on the other end of the phone asked.

"I have a dead man in my apartment," Sue answered, her voice sounding shrill.

"Are you sure that he's dead?" the woman asked.

"I'm pretty sure," Sue answered.

"Did you try CPR?"

"No, I don't know how," Sue was near hysteria.

"I'll walk you through it. First, what's your address?"

Sue gave her the information.

The woman instructed Sue on the CPR. She tried and tried, nothing was happening.

"Keep trying until the paramedics arrive," the woman instructed.

"Do you know how he died?" she asked.

"I'm not sure. I woke up this morning and he was lying next to me, dead." Sue was fighting back the tears.

"Just stay on the phone with me, the ambulance will be there in a few minutes. Can you tell me his name?"

"Randy, Randy Decker."

"Can you tell me what happened?" the woman asked.

"Nothing, he was just lying here, dead."

Sue could here the ambulance pull up in front of her building.

"They're here now."

"Okay, you can get off the phone now."

Chapter 45

Babies are born with 300 bones, but by adulthood the number is reduced to 206.

Sue tried to compose herself as the mass of medics and cops took over her tiny apartment. Two police officers immediately escorted Sue to her tiny deck to question her. She watched in horror as the EMTs tried to revive her young lover.

"What happened?" the younger officer asked.

"I woke up this morning and he was dead," she said.

"Did he have any medical problems?"

"No, not that I know of."

"How long have you known the victim?"

The victim? Oh my God! Randy was nothing more than a corpse now, a victim! "Three or four months," she replied, trying not to cry.

"Was there any drug use? Alcohol use?" the cop asked.

Sue thought she had better answer these questions very carefully. "We drank some vodka last night. If there were any drugs, I wasn't aware of them."

The police wrote down everything Sue said.

"We're going to be doing an autopsy for cause of death. We will need to take you downtown for questioning and drug testing."

Oh shit! Sue hadn't thought about that.

"Your apartment is now considered a crime scene. Our team will be here for several hours collecting evidence."

Sue just prayed that they wouldn't look under her tiny deck.

"Can I call a lawyer?" Sue asked.

"I think you should," one of the officers replied.

Sue had no idea who to call, so she called her boss at B's.

"Can you recommend a good lawyer?" Sue asked.

"What kind of lawyer?"

"Criminal," Sue responded.

"Oh," the woman answered.

The woman gave Sue the information that she needed.

"By the way, I don't think I'm going to be in to work for a few days," Sue added.

"Anything you want to tell me, Sue?"

"No, not really. Not yet anyway."

Sue called the attorney and asked him to meet her at the courthouse in an hour.

"Is it all right if I brush my teeth and change my clothes?" Sue asked the officer.

"Sorry, this is a crime scene; you can't touch anything."

Two officers escorted Sue to the back of their squad car. Sue felt as if she were watching a movie of someone else's life. This couldn't possibly be happening to her.

Chapter 46

By the age of 60, most people will have lost about half their taste buds.

It was Sue's first ride in a squad car and her first time at a police station, both experiences she could have done without.

She was led to a small office and told to wait. Her mind raced as she waited for her interrogation. She felt sick every time that she thought of poor Randy. His family was going to be heartbroken, she thought. She tried to put herself in Randy's mother's shoes, trying to imagine that it was Kevin who had died of a drug overdose.

Sue looked disheveled in a pair of navy blue Capri sweats and a plain white t-shirt. She had no bra, underwear or makeup. Her hair was still formed by the shape of her pillow from the night before. It was the first morning that she had missed her little red pill since starting with the product trial.

A plain-clothes officer finally arrived to question Sue.

"Miss Kent, I'm detective Billings. I'm going to ask you a lot of questions and we are going to examine you for evidence. We will be running a drug test as well."

"I want my attorney to be present. He should be here any moment."

"That is your right, Ms. Kent. May I offer a cup of coffee and a donut while you wait?"

"Yes please, Detective. I'm starving."

The detective returned with the refreshments and excused himself. "I will return after your attorney gets here," he said.

Sue quietly sipped on the bitter coffee as she contemplated the enormity of her situation.

An officer opened the door, "Your attorney is here, Ms. Kent."

Sue was taken off guard by the handsome face of the man in the neatly pressed, dark gray suit. "Roger Grayson, nice to meet you. I've brought you a few items to make you more comfortable while you're here." He handed Sue a small duffel bag packed with a toothbrush, toothpaste, a brush and some fresh clothes.

"Thank you so much." Sue was embarrassed to be meeting such a good-looking, sophisticated, older man in a police station while she looked like such a mess! His steel gray eyes seemed to look right through her. She found it difficult to look away.

"You have my complete discretion, Miss Kent. Please tell me what happened, and don't leave out anything."

"I had been dating Randy for the past few months. It was a pretty casual relationship. Recreational drug use was part of our experience."

"What kind of drug use?" he asked.

"The usual: pot, coke, Molly, hashish, she responded matter of factly.

"Was there anything unusual about last night?" he asked.

"Yes, as a matter of fact, there was," she answered.

"Well? What was it?" he asked.

Sue lowered her eyes to the ground. "We tried black tar heroin for the first time," Sue looked up to see her attorney's response.

"It was his idea," she continued. "He told me that it was safe if we smoked it. Sounds pretty stupid now."

"Yes, it does. Who bought it?"

"He did," she said

"Do you know where he got it?" Grayson asked.

Sue shook her head from side to side.

"Do you know if it was his first time?"

"I have no idea," Sue shook her head again.

"I want you to deny everything, Sue. Do not admit to your drug use last night. They will be taking a blood test. We'll deal with that when the time comes. For now, you had no idea about his drug use, okay?"

Sue nodded her head up and down.

"I'll see what I can do about getting you out of here. You let me worry about everything from now on. I will take care of everything."

Somehow, Sue believed him. "Thank you, Roger." Sue stood and he shook her hand firmly with a strong grip.

Chapter 47

Your eyes are always the same size from birth but your
nose and ears never stop growing.

Roger left the small office and stopped to talk to the
officer in charge. Sue watched quietly through the
window. She wondered what they were saying.

10 minutes later, Roger returned to the room.

"Sue, they are ready to photograph you and take some
blood samples. Don't be afraid. They are looking for track
marks and other signs of drug use."

"What if the blood test shows drug usage?" Sue asked
nervously.

"I will deal with that. Don't worry. Just comply with
their requests and let's get you out of here as soon as
possible."

Sue nodded in agreement.

"I will be here the whole time, just to make sure that
nothing unexpected occurs."

"Thank you," Sue said gratefully, focusing in on Roger's clear, gray eyes.

The officer questioned Sue for an hour and checked her arms for track marks. She was led to a different room and a vial of blood was taken from her arm.

"You are free to go for now, Ms. Kent. Please don't leave town. We may have more questions for you," the officer said.

"When will the blood test results be back?" Roger asked.

"We should have them by tomorrow afternoon," he said as he handed Roger his business card. "Call me at this number after four o'clock."

"Will do," Roger replied.

"Ready?" Roger asked Sue.

"Yes! Please! Get me out of here," she said eagerly.

"I'll make sure that you get home safely," he said as he placed his strong hand on the middle of her back.

Sue felt safe with him and she trusted him implicitly.

They walked up the staircase to Sue's small apartment.

"Mind if I come in for awhile so we can chat?" he asked.

"Of course, come in. Please excuse the mess. It was rather chaotic in here this morning."

Sue looked at the empty bed with sheets and pillows in disarray. She felt sick as she thought about Randy and how he had been alive in that bed just hours ago.

"Mind if I take a quick shower?" she asked.

"Take your time," he said, as he looked around the small space.

Sue reappeared moments later in a fresh pair of faded jeans, white t-shirt and with her wet hair in a towel.

"Would you like some tea?" she asked.

"Sure, that would be nice," Roger replied.

The two sat at her small, high kitchen table and sipped their tea.

"I just want to make sure that you're going to be all right, Sue."

Sue was lost in his gaze. His eyes were so familiar, so knowing and kind.

"I'll be fine," she said.

"Isn't there someone that you would like to call? Maybe a girlfriend or family member who could come over to keep you company?"

"No, there's no one," Sue said with her head down.

"Are you going to be okay here by yourself?" Roger asked.

"Yes, I'm fine. Thank you for asking."

"Call me if you need anything, Sue. I'll be back to check on you in the morning. Get some sleep tonight," he suggested.

"Yes, I'll try to do that," she said. Sue could not get over how considerate and kind Roger was being.

"Lock the door behind me and don't talk to anyone! We want to keep this story quiet. You don't need a big media scandal."

"Okay, Roger. Thank you. I'll see you tomorrow."

Chapter 48

Right-handed people live, on average, nine years longer
then left-handed people do."

Sue took a deep breath as she closed the door behind
Roger. Now what, she wondered?

She took the towel off her head and combed her thick
red hair. Time for a new look, she thought as she looked at
herself in the mirror. She phoned a local salon, making an
appointment for the following week.

Sue searched for the plastic bag that she had hidden
under her deck. She pulled out the bottle of red pills and
sat on the sofa. She held the bottle in her hand and stared
at the plastic container.

She contemplated all of the changes that had occurred
since she started on those little pills. Now, someone was
dead. She had already missed a day; maybe it was time to
stop her crazy life and go back to her old life as Sue, the

middle aged divorcee. Being beautiful was fun for a while, but seemed to be causing much more pain than pleasure. She hastily made her way to her small bathroom and quickly flushed the remains down the toilet. Doctor Elmhurst was going to be really mad, she thought.

Sue's photographer friend called. "Need anything?" He asked.

Time to stop that too, Sue thought. "No, thanks. I'm good."

She had been in a fog for so many months; she was ready to see the world clearly for a change. Death can have a very sobering effect on a person, she concluded.

Sue stripped the bed and threw the sheets into a garbage bag. She never wanted to see those sheets again, the sheets that Randy had died on.

She cleaned her small apartment from top to bottom and called for Chinese delivery.

She watched old movies and fell asleep on her sofa by 9:30.

There was a knock on the door at 8:00. It was Roger, holding two cups of coffee and a small paper bag.

"Coffee and croissants?" he asked.

Sue was happy to see his friendly face.

"Please come in, Roger. Is this normally part of an attorney's duties?" she asked, smiling.

"No, I just feel sort of paternal towards you. You remind me of my daughter and I want to make sure that you're okay."

He thought of her as a daughter? Sue was disappointed. She found herself becoming very attracted to Roger.

"How do I remind you of your daughter?" Sue asked.

"You don't look like her or anything. It's your age and the fact that you seem a little lost in life," he said.

Sue blushed. He already had her pegged as a lost soul. How right he was!

"What do you mean, lost?" She asked coyly.

132

"All the drug use. I'm sorry if I'm over-stepping my bounds here, but what was that all about? You have everything: good looks, intelligence, and a good job. Why in the world were you experimenting with so many drugs?" he asked.

"It's a very long story. The drugs are all new to me. I guess you could call it a phase. It's over now."

"I'm glad to hear that," he said, sounding relieved. "You could have been dead too, you know."

The two sat at Sue's tiny deck table sipping the coffee and getting to know one another.

Roger thanked her for the conversation and excused himself as he was expected at the office.

"Talk to you later?" she asked as her heart fluttered.

"Yes, of course. I'll call you this afternoon with the results of your blood tests."

"Oh, thanks," Sue answered, disappointed.

Chapter 49

Over 90% of diseases are caused or complicated by stress.

Sue called her children and Margie. She needed to connect. Everything was good and Karen was anxious to know when her mother would be home to help with the wedding plans.

"Soon, I promise. I'm working on it. There are still some things that I need to wrap up before I can come home."

"I can't wait, Mom. I miss you so much."

"Me too, Karen. Me too."

Sue contemplated the changes that were about to take place as her body adjusted to the changes of being off the product. It had only been two days and Sue could already feel a subtle difference. She had made her decision and now she would have to live with it.

Roger called at 4:20.

"I have your test results," he said.

Sue's heart raced, not knowing what to expect or what the consequences would be as a result.

"You're clean," he said.

Sue breathed a sigh of relief. Dr. Elmurst had been right. Every day her body was given new cells, a clean slate.

"They're calling Randy's death an accidental overdose. You are not associated with his death. You're in the clear."

"Thank you, Roger. Thank you so much," she said enthusiastically.

"You're welcome. How about a celebratory dinner? Pick you up in a hour?" he asked.

"That would be great!"

Sue was putting on her makeup when the phone rang again. It was her boss from B's.

"Sue, I don't like having to make this call, but…we're going to have to let you go."

Sue was taken off guard. "Let go, but why?"

"The incident at your apartment the other night. It doesn't reflect well on our company to have our spokesperson wake up with a drug overdosed boyfriend in her bed."

"I can see your point," Sue said.

"I'm sorry, Sue. It cost us a lot of money to keep this out of the papers."

"I understand. Thank you for the opportunity that you gave me," she said.

Sue realized that she wouldn't have been able to keep her job long anyway, now that she was off of the product. It would have only been a matter of time before they fired her for looking too old.

Sue dressed conservatively in a pair of khaki colored cashmere blend slacks, cashmere sweater and a simple strand of large baroque pearls; all from her favorite little boutique. She wore soft, muted makeup and flattened her hair to look smooth and soft. She was looking forward to her evening with Roger.

Chapter 50

A human head remains conscious for about 15 to 20 seconds after it has been decapitated.

Roger arrived right on time. He had changed out of his usual suit and tie into a pair of dress pants, dress shirt and black v-neck sweater. Sue found him to be sexy and attractive.

Roger was surprised to see his client dressed so conservatively. He was most pleased.

"I made reservations at a little French place nearby."

"Great, I love French food," Sue added.

They walked the few blocks to the restaurant. Roger ordered a bottle of wine.

"Are you old enough? I've forgotten if you're 20 or 21."

"Yes, I'm old enough. I have an ID." If he only knew, she thought.

"An interesting thing happened this afternoon," Sue started.

"Really, what was that?" Roger asked, interested.

"I was fired from B's," she said.

He looked completely surprised.

"Do you want to fight it?" he asked.

"No, I see their point. I wasn't good for their image. It's time for me to move on anyway."

"What do you have in mind?" he asked.

"Nothing yet. I just know that it's time for a change, that's all."

"I hate to bring this up, but Randy's parents have requested to meet with you."

"They what?" Sue asked, shocked.

"They have questions, they want to know what happened to their son."

"I don't know if I could face them," Sue said honestly.

Sue thought about how she would feel if she were in their shoes and it was Kevin who had died. She would want answers as well. "I'll do it," she said. "Tell Randy's parents that I will meet with them. Will you go with me?" She asked.

"Of course, that's what I'm here for. I'll set up the meeting."

"Well, here's to being unemployed," Roger said as he clinked her glass.

"So, tell me about yourself, Roger. You already know too much about me. Now I want to know more about you."

"I'm originally from Georgia. I've been a lawyer forever. I have two children, a boy and a girl, both out of college. I was married until my wife died several years ago."

"What happened? How did she die?" Sue asked, concerned.

"Breast cancer. It hit her pretty suddenly. It's been rough on all of us."

"I'm so sorry, Roger."

"I've been raising money for breast cancer ever since Lisa's death. In fact, we're having a fundraiser this weekend. You should come. We're riding bikes around the Blue Ridge Parkway."

"I don't have much experience riding," she said.

"You don't need much. Come on. It will be fun!"

"Okay, I'm in!" Sue raised her glass.

The two enjoyed a leisurely dinner. Roger walked her back to her apartment.

"Thank you for a nice evening, Sue. It was nice to have some company for a change."

"Thank you, Roger, for everything," she kissed him on the cheek.

"See you on Saturday," he said.

"Saturday!"

Sue went to bed wondering what she would say to Randy's parents.

Chapter 51

As you age, your eye color gets lighter.

Sue awakened the following morning and went directly to the nearest bicycle store. She purchased a top-of-the-line road bike, helmet, clips, shoes, socks, bike shorts, cycling tops, gloves, a bike rack and a customized seat. She had no idea how to ride. She had only ridden a bike in spin class and that did not require any balance skills.

She had three days to learn how to ride before the fundraiser on Saturday. Sue drove to a remote, flat area near Hendersonville and made her first attempt at riding a bicycle. She could barely figure out how to get the bike off the rack and her shoes in the clips, let alone ride without falling over.

Sue spent a frustrating afternoon, going no further than a few dozen feet before falling over, but she was determined not to give up. She stopped by the bike shop on her way home.

Relinquishing her pride, she asked, "Is there anyone here who can teach me to ride a bike?"

The salesman looked surprised. "You've never ridden?" he asked.

"No, never, and I only have two days left to learn."

"I could take you, I guess," the young man said. "Meet me here at 9:00 and we'll spend a few hours until you get the hang of things. Bring a pair of plain tennis shoes."

"Thank you! What's your name? You have no idea how grateful I am!"

"I'm Patrick," said the young, slim fair-haired man.

Sue spent the entire evening reading articles about bike riding and watching YouTube videos. She was going to look like a competent rider by Saturday even if it killed her!

She arrived back at the bike store at 9:00A.M. sharp in all of her riding gear.

"Follow me," Patrick said as he slipped into the driver's seat of his light green Volvo with his bike attached to the top of the vehicle.

Sue followed behind for ten minutes up Merrimon Avenue to the north side of town. Patrick pulled over near Beaver Lake and signaled for Sue to pull behind him.

Patrick patiently disengaged the bikes from their racks and proceeded to change Sue's clips for the original pedals that came with the bike.

"You can use the clips once you get the hang of things, but for now let's start with the basics," he explained.

Sue listened intently, following all of his instructions. The day was dark and overcast; Sue was bundled in an oversized gray hoodie.

Patrick asked Sue to stand next to the bike so that he could adjust the seat height. He explained the general mechanics of the bike: gears and brakes. She was ready for a trial run.

Sue sat on the high seat as Patrick gave her a little shove from behind. Sue took off and never looked back. She made it the entire way around the small man-made lake without stopping. Patrick was grinning when she returned.

"You're a natural!" he said.

"I love it! Can I go again?" she asked like an eager small child.

"Of course! Go!" Patrick said.

Sue made another loop around the lake, this time a little faster.

"That was great, Sue, now I'm going to go with you and coach you," he said.

Sue stripped the hoodie from her back and enthusiastically started on her third trip around the small lake. Patrick rode beside her, instructing her about when to change gears and cadence. After their tenth time around, Patrick suggested that he replace the clips so that Sue could see how they felt. She liked the way the clips made her ride more smooth and powerful.

"You are the most natural rider I've ever seen!"

"You never would have guessed that if you had seen me yesterday!" she said.

"I think you're fine on your own now. Do you mind if I go now?"

"Not at all. I think I have the hang of it. Thank you so much!" She handed Patrick two twenty-dollar bills.

Sue rode her new bike until dusk.

Chapter 52

The longest living cells in the body are brain cells which can live an entire lifetime.

Sue was exhausted from her first day of bike riding. It had been four days since her last little red pill, but she felt good.

She took a long, hot bath and went to bed at 8:00.

Sue was up bright and early. She loaded her new bike onto the back of her car and headed up to the Blue Ridge Parkway. She had packed a lunch and had filled her CamelBak to the brim. She was prepared for a full day of riding.

She tenaciously rode the exact path that the competitors would be riding the following day. She wanted to know the road backwards and forwards. She enjoyed the vegetation along the parkway, she wasn't used to seeing trees like oak and hickory or shrubs like rhododendron and dogwoods. The mountains were much smoother and smaller that the Sierras that she was used to seeing in Reno. She rode until her legs were numb and she was left without an ounce of strength.

Starving from her long day of riding, she stopped at Greenlife Grocery on the way home and loaded up on nutritious foods for dinner.

After a long, hot shower and some food, she fell fast asleep.

Sue felt confident in her riding abilities as she arrived the following morning at the Breast Cancer event. She spotted Roger right away. Her heart skipped a beat the moment that she saw him in his skintight riding gear. He motioned for Sue to join him.

"You look great, Sue. Are you ready for this today? We should be starting in about 10 minutes."

"I'm ready!" she said.

The sun was hot and Sue was ready to get on with the ride.

Roger made an announcement, thanking everyone for their participation.

Three hours later, the ride was over and Sue had managed to complete the 60-mile track with 300 other riders. She was most pleased with herself.

"Thanks for participating, Sue. We had a great turnout," he said.

"I enjoyed it. Thanks for inviting me," she said honestly.

"How about dinner tonight?" Roger asked.

Sue blushed, "That would be wonderful."

"Pick you up at seven?"

"Yes, see you then, Roger."

Chapter 53

Life expectancy has gone down over the past 40 years. A Russian male today can expect to live an average of 58 years.

Sue felt wonderfully exhausted after her day of riding. She was sore and sunburned. It had been six days since her last little red pill. She noticed a few faint differences. Her muscles were definitely not recovering from exercise as quickly as they had a week ago!

She showered and dressed in a bright teal and orange sundress, another one of her favorites from her shopping spree in Asheville. She blew her still-red hair straight and accessorized with several large pieces of bold turquoise jewelry.

Roger arrived on time wearing a pair of khaki shorts, a navy polo shirt and a well worn, but well taken care of pair of brown loafers. He was tan and clean.

"I made reservations for us at Fig. Have you ever been?"
Sue shook her head from side to side.

Roger drove the short distance to Biltmore in his cherry condition Mercedes sedan. They were seated at a small table outside. Roger ordered a cold bottle of Pinot Grigio.

Sue started the conversation, eager to learn more about Roger.

"So tell me more about yourself, Roger. I don't very little about you."

"There's not much to tell. I was born and raised in Atlanta. My parents divorced when I was young. I have a younger sister who still lives in Atlanta. My parents are both gone."

"I went to University of Georgia for my undergraduate degree, then to Emory for my law degree. I met my wife, Lisa, there."

"She was from Asheville, so we moved here after I graduated. We had two children, a boy and a girl. Lisa passed away three-and-a-half years ago. That's my life in a nutshell."

"I'm sure that there's a lot more to the story," Sue added.

"I don't like talking about myself very much. I'd rather hear about you," he said with a smile.

Hmmm, how would Sue tell her life story?

"I'm from Reno. I came here to model for B's and, as you know, I've been a little lost lately."

"Why is that? I'm concerned about you, you know."

"I've been meaning to ask you about that. Do you always take such a personal interest in your clients?" Sue asked.

Roger chuckled. "No, not at all. I just feel some sort of connection with you. I can't explain it."

"I know what you mean," Sue said. "You don't need to worry about me. No more drugs, I promise. Randy's death really woke me up."

"I'm glad to hear that. Now that you've lost your job, what are your plans?"

"I've decided to head back to Reno as soon as I get things squared away here."

"I'll be sorry to see you go. I hope that I can see you again before you go," he said. "I almost forgot to tell you. I heard from Randy's parents. They want to see you Tuesday afternoon. We'll make the meeting as short as possible," Roger assured her.

Sue gulped. "Okay, I guess I'm as ready as I will ever be," she said, lying. "I'm so glad that you will be there with me," she added honestly.

"You will be fine, I promise. Let's enjoy our dinner."

They ate their food, both deep in thought.

Chapter 54

Older adults are more likely to activate both hemispheres
of the brain at the same time.

Monday morning Sue called her realtor and asked him to
list her apartment, completely furnished. She called Karen
and informed her that she would be home in about a
month. They would have a full five months to plan the
wedding together.

She also called Kevin, who was fully immersed in his
own life, but relieved that his mother was coming home.

Sue made it to her hair appointment and had her hair
died back to it's natural black. She asked to have it cut to a
simple, straight shoulder length.

Tuesday morning arrived and Sue was nervous about her
meeting Randy's parents. She still had no idea what she
was going to say to them. She arrived at Roger's office a
little before the scheduled meeting, as suggested by Roger.

"Are you okay?" he asked.

"Not really," Sue said honestly.

"Well, at least your hair looks good," he said with a smile.

Sue giggled. Roger had succeeded at putting Sue at ease.

"Take a deep breath, Sue; everything will be fine."

Mr. and Mrs. Decker arrived ten minutes early.

"This is Miss Kent," Roger said, introducing the couple to Sue.

Sue extended her hand, not knowing what to expect. The couple politely shook hands with Sue, obviously fighting back tears. Everyone took a seat in Roger's comfortable office.

"Please tell us what happened that night," Randy's mother began.

"Well, we had been out to the clubs that night, dancing and drinking," Sue said.

"Did you normally do that?" Randy's father asked. "I'm sorry, we didn't know much about Randy's life."

Sue looked surprised. She composed herself and answered, "Yes, we went out most nights."

"How long had you known my son?" Randy's mother asked.

"A few months."

"I'm sorry for interrupting, please continue with the story," his mother said.

Sue watched the couple as they tried to contain their emotions, both were wiping tears from their eyes as Sue spoke.

"We had been drinking vodka and snorting cocaine," Sue said, watching for their reaction. "That night, Randy had brought some black tar heroin to my apartment."

Randy's mother gasped.

"At first I didn't want to try it, but Randy assured me that smoking it was perfectly safe. We smoked a little and went to bed, and that was it; he never woke up."

Randy's mother began sobbing.

Roger interjected, "Please continue, Sue."

"I'm so sorry, it's all my fault! I'm the one who should have died that night! Please forgive me!" Sue began sobbing as well.

"We don't blame you, we blame ourselves. We were so busy fighting with each other that we couldn't see what was happening to Randy. We were in the process of getting a divorce, and he took it really hard. That's when he started using drugs," his father said.

Sue stopped crying and listened.

"We just wanted to know what happened to our boy on the last night of his life," his father continued. "We can't thank you enough for giving us that."

Sue nodded, with tears rolling down her face.

The couple thanked Roger for his time and said goodbye.

Roger asked, "Are you all right, Sue? You did a great job."

He hugged her and she sobbed quietly on his shoulder. "I feel so guilty. Randy died because of me. If I hadn't agreed to smoke the heroin that night, he would still be here and that nice couple wouldn't have lost their only son."

"It's over now. You need to get on with your life now, Sue. You need to stay far away from drugs."

"I will, I promise." This time she meant it.

Chapter 55

Biological age does not equal chronological age.

It had now been over a week since her last little red pill and Sue was feeling the effects. She wasn't waking as quickly in the morning and her muscles were definitely becoming sorer from all of the bike riding. Her hair and nails weren't growing as quickly. She still felt good though, and full of energy.

Dr. Elmhurst was going to be very unhappy that Sue had stopped taking the pills. She had no idea what the repercussions would be for stopping the program, but she had done what she had to do. Randy's death was a constant reminder of her mistakes.

Sue had a plan in mind. She needed to age quite a bit before returning to Reno and seeing her family, so she decided to take her time driving back to Nevada.

She passed hours on the computer researching places to bike ride across the country. She plotted a course that would take her a month to reach Reno.

Sue called Margie and broke the news to her that she was coming home.

"Really?" she asked, "Are you really coming home?" she was crying.

"Yes, I really miss you, Margie. I hope that we will be able to resume our friendship."

"That would be wonderful," Margie replied.

She decided not to call John, who was still pestering her with text messages on a regular basis.

After a week of preparation, it was time for Sue to leave Asheville. She realized that there was only one person to whom she had to say goodbye: Roger. Her time in Asheville had been sad and lonely. It was definitely time to move on and do something constructive with her life.

She packed her few belongings in her Lexus SUV. Her clothes wouldn't be fitting her soon and the only thing that she cared about now was her new bike and biking gear.

She called Roger and asked him to meet her for a farewell dinner.

Chapter 56

The brain never stops growing.

Roger picked up Sue on her last night in Asheville. Sue dressed in one of her new outfits, a beige lace short skirt with a complimenting silk blouse. She looked elegant with simple, classic pearl jewelry and a pair of high-heeled sandals.

Roger barely recognized his dinner companion.

"You look so different," he said, "but you do almost every time I see you. I like your hair color: it compliments the blue of your eyes."

Sue loved the flattery, "Thank you, Roger," she replied gratefully.

"How does Mediterranean sound tonight? Okay with you?" he asked.

"That sounds wonderful," Sue replied.

They were seated at a quiet table for two. Roger ordered a bottle of Malbec and asked Sue about her plans. She couldn't exactly tell him that she had to age a bit before going home to help her 25-year-old daughter prepare for her wedding!

"I thought that I would take my time going back. I'd like to get in as many rides as I can along the way. Who knows when I will have the opportunity again to ride across the country?"

"You really have taken to riding, haven't you?" Roger asked.

"I don't think I've ever been as enthusiastic and passionate about anything in my life, and I have you to thank for it," Sue responded honestly.

"Me? Why?" Roger asked.

"I have a confession to make. I had never ridden a bicycle before in my life until the week before the breast cancer event."

"Really?" Roger laughed. "I never would have guessed! You look like you've been racing all of your life."

"Thank you. I got a late start, but I hope to ride for the rest of my life," Sue said.

"I love it too. I go every chance that I get, usually after work every night and on the weekends. There just never seems to be enough time," he said.

"So, what will you do when you get back to Reno?" he asked.

"I don't really know yet," Sue answered.

"You're awfully young; you have plenty of time to figure it out."

If he only knew! Sue thought.

Sue studied Roger's face throughout the evening, thinking that this was, perhaps, the last time that she would ever see him.

"Thank you for everything, Roger. You saved me and you've been so kind. You're the only friend that I've made while I've been here in Asheville."

"Certainly, that can't be true. What about friends you've made at B's or friends that you had with Randy?"

"There were none. You're it," she said.

"Well, I am honored to be your friend, Sue. I hope to hear from you and I wish you nothing but the best in your life."

The two exchanged contact information and promised to keep in touch. Sue felt sad and lonely as she said goodbye to her only friend.

Chapter 57

Reasoning and problem-solving skills get sharper with age.

Sue set out early the following morning. It was early September and the air was crisp. She took I-40 and headed west toward Tennessee with her bike on the back of her dark gray SUV.

She drove four-and-a-half hours to Nashville and checked into the Best Western. She had the entire afternoon left to ride. Sue had preplanned her route. She returned to the hotel at dusk and woke early in the morning to explore a different route. She spent a second night in Nashville before resuming her drive to the next destination – Indianapolis.

Sue continued the pattern, taking time to enjoy her environment and to clear her head. It was the first time that she had consciously contemplated her life since beginning on the program.

Her life became clear as she rode for hours each day. She recalled the depression of her life before the program and the exhilaration of the newness of life as she started on the product.

Sue realized that she had given no thought to her actions along the way; she had just become lost, going deeper and deeper into a hole of emptiness.

The drugs were an escape, as was Sofia. It was the horror of Randy's death that finally snapped her out of her downward spiral, then meeting Roger and being inspired by his kindness and honor.

It became clear to her that what mattered in life were her children and riding. That was all that mattered now, and hopefully, to see Roger again one day.

As Sue rode each day, her head became clearer and clearer. She was also painfully aware that her body was becoming older with each passing day.

The wrinkles were reappearing and the weight was slowly returning. She was determined to stay off of the product and return to her old life as a better, happier and healthier Sue.

She called her children and Margie each night feeling the anticipation and excitement of their reunion.

By the time she arrived in Reno, Sue had logged 1,000 miles on her bicycle. Her face had aged, but her body was in great shape.

Chapter 58

Older individuals are able to focus on the upside.

Sue pulled her SUV into her driveway on Ambassador Drive, where she hadn't stepped foot in over six months. She had an eerie feeling as she parked her car, as if, somehow, the past six months hadn't really happened. She hadn't taken the drugs, had sex with Sofia and all of those men and that Randy really hadn't died, but he had and she would never be able to escape that reality.

The house looked just the same as she stepped inside. Karen must have had it cleaned as there was no dust or dirt anywhere.

Sue was anxious and nervous as she dialed her children to tell them that she was home.

"I'm here," she said to Karen.

"Here, here?" Karen asked.

"Yes, I'm home. Please come over."

She called Kevin as well.

Her stomach was in knots as she studied her face in the mirror. She guessed that she looked to be somewhere in her late 30's. She hoped that she looked old enough for her children to accept her. At least she didn't look 20 any more!

Karen arrived first. She burst through the front door.

"Mom, I can't believe that you're really here!" Karen hugged her tightly. "Let me look at you. You look good, Mom, really healthy!"

"You look great too, Honey. You look happy," Sue added.

"Is that your SUV in the driveway? What's with the bicycle?"

"Yes, the car is mine and so is the bike. I've taken up cycling while I was gone."

"Really? Good for you, Mom. I never know what you're going to do next!" Karen exclaimed.

Kevin pulled up in his small, white Dodge pickup truck. He cried the moment that he saw Sue. He hugged her as hard as he could.

"I missed you so much, Mom. I thought that you were never coming back."

Sue tried to hold back the tears, "I'm sorry for what I've put you through. I'm here now, though, and I'm not going anywhere."

"So, Mom, tell us where you've been. What have you been doing all of these months?" Kevin asked.

Sue cringed. There was no way that she could tell him the truth; that she had been using drugs, sleeping around and had waked up with a dead man!

"It's a long, boring story. I'd rather hear about what's been going on with you."

Sue's children were only too happy to share the details of their lives while she had been away. Sue listened patiently, thrilled to be back with her children whom she had missed more than had she ever realized.

Chapter 59

People skills are constantly improving with age.

Sue slowly resumed her old life. She contacted Margie and asked her to meet for lunch. Sue wore little makeup and loose clothing, hoping to look a little older than her present age. Margie was obviously guarded as she talked to Sue.

"I don't know if I can trust you," Margie started.

"That will take time," Sue said. "I know that I've hurt you. My actions lately have nothing to do with you. Please let me make it up to you."

"Let's just see how it goes," Margie said.

"Fair enough," Sue responded.

"So, tell me about your adventures while you've been gone." Margie added.

There was no way that Sue was going to tell Margie anything about her life in Asheville!

"I started cycling," Sue said innocently.

"Really? That's a surprise. What about your modeling career? That must have been exciting."

"No, not really. It was a lot of work. I'm not doing it any more."

"Why not? It sounded like a dream job! What will you do now? Go back to the law office?" Margie asked.

What a horrible thought! Sue concluded. "No, I don't know what I'm going to do yet. I still have a lot to work out. The most important thing is Karen's wedding."

Margie changed the subject to all of the gossip that Sue had missed while she was gone. Sue pretended to listen as her mind wandered to the events of her life in Asheville. She smiled as she thought of Roger and his handsome face. She missed him.

John appeared at Sue's door that evening.

Sue was in her biking gear, getting ready to go to spin class.

"I'm so glad that you're home," he said. "The kids told me that you were here. I could hardly believe it. I've been waiting for you, Sue. You look great, so different…again."

Sue sighed, "John, I've told you not to wait for me. There is no 'us'! Get on with your life, I have."

"I'm not giving up, Sue; you'll see that we belong together," he said as he walked out the door.

Sue went to her spin class and lost herself in her thoughts. She wanted to make this life work for her, but she just hadn't quite figured out how yet.

Chapter 60

A new study suggests that low cholesterol levels are associated with mortality from cardiovascular disease.

Karen had preparations for her wedding well under way. The wedding and reception were planned for the nearby Somersett Country Club. Karen's guest list included 100 guests. She needed her mother's help picking out a dress, bridesmaids' dresses, flowers, invitations, and music.

The dress was first on the list. Mother and daughter made the rounds to a half dozen bridal shops. The two women agreed on a satin, strapless, full-length mermaid style dress to show off Karen's hourglass figure, with layers of organza at the bottom.

The three bridesmaids would be wearing form-fitting knee length, strapless sky blue dresses of satin and taffeta. All three bridesmaids had the figures to pull off the revealing dresses.

Karen was thrilled to have her mother at her side for such an important day. The two women celebrated by having a special lunch at Rapscallion. Sue ordered her favorite shrimp Caesar salad with extra anchovies. She was happy to be back in her daughter's life.

"Are you and Daddy going to be able to get along for the wedding?" Karen asked.

"I don't see why not. I have no problem with your father," Sue answered.

"Yes, but Daddy's obsessed with you. He left Brittany for you. He's going to expect to be your date for the wedding."

"Don't worry about that, Karen. I will handle your father." Sue had no idea how she was going to do that.

On the way home they stopped at Michael's and found some elegant invitations. Karen would address the invitations by hand, using the calligraphy techniques that she had learned in high school.

Karen dropped her mother off on her way home.

"Thanks for today, Mom. It's great to have you back."

"It's great to be back," she answered.

Sue took another spin class that night and her mind wandered to thoughts of Roger again. She knew that she would never see him again; how could she? The Sue that he knew was already a much older woman. There would be no way to explain things.

Margie had left a message on Sue's phone inviting her to Rum Bullions the following night. Sue had no interest in going, but knew that she must to keep the relationship going with her friend.

Chapter 61

Anger, stress and worry become less common in old age.

Sue spent the day riding. She put in a full eight hours. It was a perfect fall day for riding. She arrived home in time to shower and get ready to meet the girls at Rum Bullions.

The girls were all there when she arrived. The group welcomed Sue as she entered the bar looking like a very fit forty year old in a black satin jumpsuit with 4" high pumps and the dark stain of red on her lips. Her shoulder length black hair had been blown straight and finished off with a straightening iron.

Sue did not want to be back in the same place where her whole nightmare had started. She was reminded of how she had felt when the men at Rum Bullions became interested in her. It was a rush that she hadn't experienced in years. Now, the same situation held no excitement for her at all.

The group ordered a round of Cosmos and Sue listened dutifully as the women babbled on about the gossip in town. Sue felt like an outcast as they filled her in on the local list of divorces and affairs.

"So, when do we get to hear about what you've been up to all of these months?" One of the women asked. "I'll bet that you have some exciting stories to tell. Modeling must be so glamorous."

Sue thought about her drug use and wondered how exciting the women would find that.

"It's not nearly as glamorous as you would think," Sue answered, while picturing young Randy's dead body in her bed. "Not glamorous at all, really," she added.

The women looked at her with surprise, and then quickly changed the subject.

Several men approached Sue, asking her to dance. She declined and noticed the looks of disapproval from her group. The woman had expected Sue to dance the night away as she had done in the past.

Sue quietly finished her cocktail and politely excused herself.

"It's been a long day," she said, "I need to get to bed early tonight."

"But, you just got here," one said.

"I'm sorry, next time." Sue couldn't get out of there fast enough.

She sat in a hot tub when she got home. Her mind roamed to Roger, then to Dr. Elmhurst. Her appointment was coming up. How was she going to explain things to him? What if he insisted that she go back on the product? She had made up her mind and had to stick to it.

The evening had left Sue feeling out of sorts. Where did she fit in now? Going back to her old life wasn't working. She was happy, though, to have the most important thing back in her life, her kids. The rest would work itself out somehow.

Chapter 62

Wisdom grows with age.

Sue spent her days riding and her evenings at spin class. The spin instructor approached Sue one night after class.

"One of our instructors left and I'm in a pinch. You seem to be a very experienced rider. How would you like to take over and teach some classes?" he asked.

Sue was caught off guard, "Oh, no, I couldn't. I come here to zone out. Thank you anyway."

"Suit yourself. Let me know if you change your mind."

Sue thought about the offer when she got home and she did change her mind. She spent a couple of hours putting music together for her first class. She informed the instructor of her change of mind the following evening.

"Great! You can start tomorrow. Thanks for helping me out."

Sue was nervous for her first class. It was the first time she had seen such a full class. All of the bikes were taken and she had to teach without a bike. It was a bit of a challenge, but she managed to make her way through and found that she really enjoyed it.

The aging process was catching up with her. The wrinkles were returning as well as some of the aches and pains. She had regained some weight, perhaps 20 pounds, but the cycling was keeping her former paunch away. She still looked good, much better than she had previously at age 45.

One day she received an unexpected call from Dr. Elmhurst.

"Sue, I know that you are due to come in soon. We've had some serious problems with the program though, and we've had to shut things down. I must stress to you the continued importance of keeping quiet about our project. If you tell anyone, there will be no evidence to back you up. We've erased every trace that we ever existed."

"As long as you comply, you will receive a lifetime supply of the product. That's enough for you to take one pill every day until you reach the age of 125, but you must tell no one. We will be watching."

"I'm sorry that things worked out this way, Sue. You've been an exemplary participant and I wish you nothing but the best."

"But, Dr. Elmhurst…"

"I'm sorry, Sue. Goodbye."

Chapter 63

Married seniors report greater satisfaction with their marriages.

Sue was spending time with her children and riding. She decided to become involved with riding her bike to raise money for breast cancer. She thought about Roger and how he had inspired her to do something and participate in memory of his late wife, Lisa.

Sue traveled to San Francisco, Los Angeles, and Napa. She loved the rides, but was finding her aging body becoming more of a challenge with each day.

Unfortunately, Sue recognized the familiar changes of menopause occurring in her body, as if going through it once weren't enough! She knew that she was in for a miserable long haul of weight gain, insomnia and mood swings. She noticed that her hair was thinning and that the gray hairs were returning as well.

The energy that she'd had when she started riding in Asheville was gone and it required a greater effort every day to keep up the pace on her bicycle.

Sue made an effort to keep up her friendship with Margie, though she decided to let go of the rest of the group. She met Margie for lunch at the Grille one day.

"How would you like to try riding with me one day?" Sue asked Margie.

"I could never keep up with you!" Margie exclaimed.

"Sure you could. I'll teach you. It will be fun." Sue encouraged her.

Margie agreed reluctantly. They set a date to ride the following Saturday.

Sue met with Karen on a regular basis, trying to tie up all of the loose ends for the wedding.

They chose the flowers, the band and shopped for Sue's mother-of-the-bride dress.

Sue, at her thinnest, had been a size two and now she was back up to a six. She was very comfortable with her body at this size. They found a knee length navy A-line dress with a square neckline of lace chiffon. It was a perfect compliment to the bridesmaid's dresses. Everything was in order. All the arrangements were set at Somersett Country Club.

John called Sue a week before the wedding. "Will you be my date for the wedding, Sue? Or, do you already have a date?"

"I don't think it's a good idea, John."

"What would possibly made our daughter happier than having her parents together on her wedding day?" John stated convincingly.

"I'll think about it, John. I hadn't thought of it in that way," Sue responded.

She called her daughter. "What do you think of your father and mother going to the wedding together? Do you like the idea or not?"

"I think it's a great idea, Mom, if you can handle it," Karen said.

It was decided; Sue would attend the wedding with John, but she had a bad feeling about the whole idea.

Chapter 64

25-30% of people aged 85 or older have some degree of cognitive decline.

Sue and Margie headed out for their first ride. Sue had borrowed Kevin's bike for Margie to use. She took Margie to a flat area in Sparks.

"Don't expect much from me," Margie started. "I haven't ridden a bike in years."

"Don't worry; I had never ridden a bike in my life," Sue responded compassionately. "We're not going to go far," Sue assured her.

Sue set up the seat for Margie's height and encouraged her to mount the bike and held it for her as she took a seat.

"I'm going to wait here and watch you first, then we'll ride together," she said, remembering her first day with Patrick and how he had handled the situation.

Sue gave Margie a little push as she headed north. Margie wobbled a bit, but got the hang of it after a few minutes.

"That was great!" Sue exclaimed, "Now, let's go together."

Margie huffed and puffed while Sue encouraged her to keep going. They rode a mile out and a mile back. Margie was grinning, pleased with her achievement.

"See, you can do it!" Sue exclaimed, "Next time we will go a little further."

Sue dropped Margie at her house and spent a quiet evening at home. She was sad and lonely, still feeling like she didn't fit in anywhere.

She took off all of her clothes and gave herself a good once over in the full-length mirror. Some of the cellulite was back, and the sagging breasts and skin, but her legs and buttocks looked better than they had previously. It was a hard dose of reality. Her body was definitely back in its 50's.

Maybe she had made the wrong choice about the product. Sue missed the exhilaration of seeing a younger and slimmer version of herself every day in the mirror.

Where was the product, by the way? Dr. Elmhurst had promised her a lifetime supply in the mail. It was a good thing that she wasn't taking them.

Margie called to thank Sue for taking her riding.

"I didn't want to go, but I feel so good now. When can we go again?" She asked enthusiastically.

Sue giggled, "It's addictive, isn't it? Why don't you come to spin class with me?"

"Oh, no! That sounds way too hard."

"You made it through today, didn't you?"

Sue convinced her friend and the two started riding together several times a week with an occasional spin class thrown in. Margie wasn't quite as enthusiastic a rider as Sue was, but she did enjoy her time on the bike.

Chapter 65

A Georgian woman claims to be the oldest person alive at 131.

Karen and Gary's wedding day arrived. It was a beautiful spring day in Reno.

John picked up Sue at her small house on Ambassador Drive. She was dressed in her mother-of-the-bride gown and the strand of pearls that John had given her for their first anniversary.

"You remembered!" John exclaimed as Sue opened the door.

Sue had a confused look on her face.

"The pearls," he said, "I knew that you still loved me."

"Don't start, John."

"Whatever you say, my lovely."

Sue shot her ex a dirty look.

"Let's just get along today, John, okay?"

"Okay," he answered.

John opened the door to his blue Audi. He and Sue had arrived an hour before the wedding was to begin. Karen was busy getting dressed with her bridesmaids. The room was in disarray with women doing hair and makeup.

"Oh, Mom, you're here. You look beautiful!" Karen exclaimed.

Karen was happy to see her mom looking like a mom, not a twenty-year-old sister!

Sue cried the moment that she saw her daughter in her wedding dress. Everything that she had been through had been worth it to be here at this moment, to be with her daughter on her wedding day.

The ceremony was perfect and Sue was happy to have Gary for a son-in-law. He was good to Karen and he made her happy. That was all that mattered in Sue's mind.

The band started right after the ceremony. The first song was Bette Midler's *The Wind Beneath My Wings*. John grabbed Sue right away.

"They played this at our wedding, remember? It's a sign. We should be together!"

"John! Please!" Sue protested.

"C'mon Sue, just dance with me," he pleaded.

Sue complied to keep the peace. John twirled his ex around the dance floor, grinning from ear to ear.

"When did you learn how to dance?" Sue asked.

"Brittany made me take lessons for our wedding," he answered.

Sue enjoyed her dance partner's expertise, and at the same time couldn't wait for the song to be over.

"Thanks for the dance, John," Sue said politely. "I need to mingle with the guests. You should do the same," she suggested.

John headed straight for the bar. He ordered his third Maker's Mark on the rocks.

The family and wedding party gathered for photos. John managed to stand next to his ex-wife in every photo. Sue was becoming annoyed.

The reception lasted for four hours. Sue mingled most of the time enjoying her first encounter with some of her friends for the first time since she started on the product. She now looked like her original self, though 30 pounds lighter and more vibrant than before.

John continued to hit the bourbon and make more of a nuisance of himself to Sue. He followed her everywhere she went and continually asked her to dance.

"Enough, John! Leave me alone!" she said, finally.

John was not deterred; he only became louder and more insistent. Eventually he was crying as he begged Sue to come with him.

Two of Gary's groomsmen discreetly escorted John from the premises, putting him in a cab and instructing the driver to take him home.

"Mom, Dad almost ruined our whole reception. His behavior is an embarrassment!"

"He's gone now, Honey. Don't worry about your father. Enjoy the rest of the reception and I will deal with your father tomorrow. It's your wedding day! Enjoy!"

Chapter 66

Satisfaction with social relationships grows with age.

Karen and Gary left for their honeymoon in Hawaii. Sue did her best to settle into her life, such as it was.

Sue paid a visit to John the day after the wedding.

"That was quite a spectacle last night," she started. "You almost ruined your daughter's wedding, John."

"I know. I'm pretty ashamed of myself. I'm pretty messed up these days. My life is falling apart. Brittany left me and my business is in serious danger of going under."

"I thought you left Brittany," Sue interjected.

"That's what I wanted you to believe, Sue. She left me because I'm a mess…drinking too much," John admitted.

"It sounds like you need help, John."

"I think you're right. I'm sorry about what I've been putting you through. I fixated on you because you have been the only stability in my life over the years."

"It's okay, John. Back off on the drinking, though, okay? That never helps anything," Sue said.

John agreed to get some help.

Sue taught spin classes, rode bikes with Margie a couple of times a week and participated in fund raising rides whenever possible.

"Mom, I'd like to ride with you sometime," Kevin blurted one day out of the blue.

"Really? Where did that come from?" Sue asked.

"I've been watching how much you enjoy it. I've ridden a few times. I'd like to give it a try," he said.

"Great, why don't you come with me on Saturday? We can do a four hour ride out near Stead."

"I'm in," Kevin said without hesitation.

Sue was happy to have more time alone with her son. The riding became a great bonding experience for mother and son. Kevin was almost as hooked as his mother was. He even participated the fund raising rides.

Sue was pretty happy with her life. The only thing that really bothered her was being in her 50's again. She missed the exuberance of her temporary youth. She often wondered if she had made the right decision to go off of the product. She concluded that it didn't really matter since Dr. Elmhurst had never sent the product to her anyway, and she had no way to contact him.

Chapter 67

Happiness increases with age.

It was fall, six months after the wedding. Sue came home one evening after spin class. She had been dripping in perspiration and had pulled on her favorite hot pink sweat suit over her spin clothes.

She had just poured herself a large glass of white wine when there was a knock at the door. With a glass of wine in one hand, she opened the door with the other. Roger Grayson was standing in the doorway.

"Oh, shit!' she exclaimed, spilling wine on her arm and on the floor.

"Excuse me?" Roger asked.

"Oh, I'm sorry," Sue said trying to compose herself.

"My name is Roger Grayson," he said.

That's right, he doesn't know who I am! Sue concluded.

"I'm looking for Susan Kent. She gave me this address. I'm a friend of hers from North Carolina," he said.

"I'm so sorry," Sue stammered. "I didn't mean to be rude, I'm Sue's mother. My name is Sue as well. Please come in," she offered. Holy shit, Roger is here; now what do I do, she wondered? She tried to remain calm and cool.

"Nice to meet you, Sue. Your daughter has your eyes," he said.

If he only knew! Sue thought.

"May I offer you a glass of wine?" She asked.

"Yes, I would like that, thank you," he answered.

"Please excuse the way I look. I just came from spin class," she said apologetically.

"You ride?" he asked.

"Yes, I do." You are the one that got me started riding, she thought. "I also teach a spin class several times a week," she added.

"I ride, too, every chance that I get," he said.

"Then it looks like we have something in common," Sue commented.

The two sat in Sue's comfortable living room and sipped their wine as they continued the conversation. Sue couldn't believe that Roger Grayson was sitting in her living room after all of these months!

"That's odd," Roger said under his breath.

"What was that?" Sue asked.

"I was just thinking that it's odd that you ride so much. Sue said that she had never ridden a bike before in her life until recently."

"Oh, it's recent for me too," Sue said honestly.

"Where is she? Is she around?" Roger asked.

Blurting out the first thing that came to mind, Sue said, "She's in Europe. She was having some problems and thought it would be best to get away."

"That makes sense," Roger concluded.

Sue couldn't stop staring at Roger.

"So, what brings you here? You said that you're from North Carolina?" Sue asked innocently.

"I'm here for a ride, actually. To raise money for breast cancer," Roger said.

"I'm signed up for that race!" Sue exclaimed.

"Really? What a coincidence!"

The two chatted for hours. Sue prepared a meal of grilled chicken, Caprese salad and grilled artichokes. They polished of two bottles of wine. It was one o'clock in the morning before either of them looked at the time.

"I can't believe it's so late," Roger commented. "The evening seemed to fly by."

"Would you like to ride with me tomorrow? To warm up for the race on Saturday?" he asked.

"I would love that!" Sue answered honestly.

"I'm staying at the Atlantis. I'll come by and pick you up at eight?" he asked.

"That sounds perfect, Roger. Thank you."

Sue floated off to bed, excited that Roger was really here, really in her life.

Chapter 68

No American has officially died of 'old age' since 1951, when the government eliminated that classification on death certificates.

Roger arrived bright and early. It was a brisk autumn day and the two were bundled in layers that could be peeled off as the day progressed.

Sue was beside herself with happiness. She was going to spend the day with Roger! She had packed a picnic and was ready to go.

"I can't get over how much you and your daughter look alike," Roger commented.

"We hear that a lot," Sue said trying to contain a burst of laughter.

Sue instructed Roger where to drive. She picked Stead again, where she first took Kevin.

They chatted along the way.

"How long are you here?" Sue asked, afraid of the answer.

"I go back on Tuesday," he said. "I have a court date on Wednesday."

"Court?" Sue asked.

"Yes, I'm an attorney. That's how I met Sue. Did she ever tell you about me?"

"As a matter of fact, she did. She told me all about her drug use and that poor boy dying. It scared her straight. That's why she's in Europe now. To get her head on right," Sue said.

"I'm glad to hear that. I was really worried about her," said Roger.

"Thank you for looking out for my daughter and being so good to her," Sue said.

"It was my pleasure. I really cared about her. She seems like a really good person who was temporarily mixed up," Roger said compassionately.

"I think that sums it up perfectly," Sue agreed.

How odd it was, Sue thought, to be having this conversation with Roger about herself as if she were a different person!

The two spent the day riding. They were perfectly paired in abilities. They raced one another several times and took turns winning.

They stopped mid-afternoon to enjoy Sue's picnic. She had packed fruit, cheese, turkey and nuts.

Roger opened up about his life and his late wife's passing and and Sue pretended to hear it for the first time.

"What about you?" he asked. "Sue never told me anything about you or anyone else in your family. Do you have other kids? Are you divorced? Widowed?"

Now Sue could finally tell the truth about her life.

"Sue is my youngest," she lied, I also have a 25-year-old daughter, Karen, and a 23-year-old son, Kevin. They both live here in Reno, as does my ex, John."

They talked deeply about their lives. Sue found herself becoming even more attracted to Roger. She wondered how old he was. She was now 58.

Chapter 69

Approximately 100,000,000,000 (that's 100 billion!) have died since humans began.

Sue and Roger finished their ride at a relaxed pace. Roger asked if he could take Sue to dinner.

"That sounds wonderful," she said.

"Would you pick a place? I don't know Reno. I'll pick you up at seven?"

"I'll be ready," Sue said.

Roger dropped Sue at her house and headed back to his hotel.

Sue's head was reeling. She really cared for Roger and she didn't want to blow it with lies and running away as she had in the past.

She took a long bath and contemplated her present situation. She only had three days to solidify a relationship with Roger before he left for North Carolina.

There was obviously a connection between the two of them. He must see it as well, she hoped. How could he not see that young Sue and old Sue are one and the same?

Sue dressed carefully, knowing that Roger preferred a conservative look to a slutty one. She decided on a pair of black slacks, a tailored white blouse and John's white pearl necklace. She blew her black, shoulder length hair straight and curled it in slightly at the bottom. She chose a deep pink lipstick to off-set the deep blue of her eyes.

Roger arrived wearing dark washed jeans and a blue dress shirt. He had on a pair of cowboy boots. Sue commented on them right away.

"I never figured you for a cowboy boot kind of a guy," Sue said sarcastically.

"I just thought they would be appropriate in Reno. I've never worn them before," Roger answered, embarrassed.

"They're perfect. I made reservations at a quiet little bistro. I hope that's alright with you," Sue said.

"If you like it, I'm sure that I will too," Roger answered agreeably. "You look beautiful, by the way."

"Thank you, Roger."

The two were seated in the front room, next to the fireplace at the 4th Street Bistro.

Roger ordered a bottle of wine and started the conversation.

"Tell me about Sue," he said.

"What would you like to know?" Sue asked, curious.

"I've been wondering what led her to the mess that she was in in Asheville," said Roger.

How was she going to explain this to him, she wondered?

"She was feeling lost and lonely. She had the world by the tail, but she didn't realize it. It didn't mean anything to her. Now it does. She now knows that her drug use and floating around with no sense of direction was a big mistake. I think that she has direction and focus now."

"Are you sure that she's not getting into more trouble in Europe?" Roger asked.

"Yes, I'm quite sure," Sue giggled.

"Would you like to come to my spin class tomorrow?" Sue asked.

"I've never tried it before. It seems a little intimidating," Roger commented.

"Nonsense! If you can ride, you can easily take a spin class," Sue assured him.

"Okay, why not? I'll give it a try."

"The class is at noon and lasts for an hour."

"We'll see if I last that long," he added.

"You'll be fine; you'll see. I'll even bet that you become hooked like every else," Sue said.

"That remains to be seen," Roger said doubtfully.

Chapter 70

Eighty percent of people who die in the United States die in a hospital.

Sue had a full class. Everyone liked the music that she played in her classes, so they were usually full. Roger struggled a little, but managed to make it through the entire class.

"That was great!" Roger exclaimed as he wiped the sweat from his forehead. "I feel invigorated!"

"I told you it was addictive!"

"How about some lunch? I'm starving," Roger said.

They had burgers at PJ's and discussed the upcoming race. Sue invited Roger to her house for dinner. She dropped him at his hotel after lunch so he could nap and take a shower.

He arrived at Sue's with a bottle of wine in hand.

"Thank you!" Sue said as she took the bottle from Roger.

"Something smells wonderful," he commented as he walked through the door.

"That's garlic. I'm making shrimp scampi."

Roger opened the wine and the two sat in Sue's comfortable living room.

"I hope you don't mind that I've been monopolizing all of your time," he said.

"I've enjoyed your company. I'm glad that you're here," Sue said, thinking that she was over the moon happy that Roger was there with her.

"Tell me about your wife," Sue asked, hesitantly.

"We met when I was in graduate school. Lisa was studying to be a nurse. We fell in love immediately and were married as soon as we both finished our educations."

"The kids happened pretty quickly...faster than we had expected. We had planned to travel first, but it just didn't happen that way. We worked hard, raised our kids and had a pretty good marriage. We had hoped to travel when the kids were gone."

"Lisa's cancer started just about the time that the kids were finishing high school. There was no travel. Lisa's health declined rapidly and we tried everything to keep her alive."

"We spent three years trying every kind of alternative and traditional treatment that we could think of. Lisa was determined to live to see her kids grow into adults and to see her grandchildren."

"I found her dead in our bed one morning. I know it may sound strange, but I was surprised when she died. After that it was just the kids and me. We started traveling everywhere. I took them to Australia, Bora Bora, and every place I could think of. Every college break, we went somewhere new. Once they were out of college and working, the traveling stopped."

"I started dating about that time. I was really a wreck inside, but no one could tell. I had no business dating, really. I still had a lot of healing to do after losing Lisa."

"Wow, that's quite a lot to go through," Sue commented. She was more attracted to Roger than ever.

"That's when I decided to start raising money for breast cancer. It gave me something positive to focus on, and that's where I am now," he concluded.

"And how are your children now?" Sue asked.

"They're okay. My son is pretty quiet about his feelings and my daughter tends to be rebellious. That's why Sue reminded me so much of her," Roger concluded.

"Yes, Sue has been pretty rebellious all right," Sue agreed.

"So, we have something in common then," Roger said as he raised his wine glass in the air.

"To having things in common," Sue said as she clinked her glass against Roger's.

The two conversed until well after midnight.

"We have a race in the morning," Sue reminded him.

"Yes, we do. I'm sorry that I've kept you up late again," Roger said as he headed for the door.

"Don't be silly. I enjoyed it. See you at the race?" she asked.

"See you in the morning, Sue. Thank you for dinner, again," he said as he disappeared into the night.

Chapter 71

In the end, lack of oxygen is always the final cause of death.

Sue went to bed replaying Roger's story over and over again in her head. She thought about how devoted and compassionate he had been to his wife. The more she learned about him, the more impressed with him she became.

Sue arrived at the race on time. Roger was there getting things organized. He was talking to a young woman when Sue approached him. The two were involved in a heated conversation and Sue was ignored. She felt embarrassed standing next to Roger and overhearing the conversation between the two.

"You said that you would be in touch," the young woman said angrily.

"No, I said that I would see you around. It's different," Roger corrected her. "What are you doing here anyway? This is a long way from North Carolina," he added.

"I have every right to be here, just as much as you do," she said.

"This is not the time or place for this," Roger told the woman.

"It's never the right time or place for you, Roger," the woman said as she walked her back away from Roger in a huff.

Sue stood frozen, embarrassed, and quite jealous. What was going on between Roger and that woman, she wondered?

"Hi, Sue. Sorry about that," he said apologetically with anger in his voice.

"Anything that you want to talk about?" Sue asked.

"No, she's just someone that I used to date. She won't let things go," he said.

Roger dated her? She must be about 30! Sue was even more jealous now.

Sue's face turned bright red, but Roger didn't notice.

"Let's get this race started," Roger said, heading to the front of the line.

Sue's mind was on Roger and the young woman during the entire race. She wondered if he was only interested in young women. He hadn't made any moves on her, after all. Maybe he saw her as a companion, a friend. Now what? She only had one more day with Roger before he was due to leave for North Carolina.

Sue breezed through the race, not thinking about riding at all. She observed another interaction between Roger and the young woman when the race was over, though she couldn't make out what they were saying.

"Thanks for participating, Sue," he said flatly.

"I've got some things to take care of tonight. Why don't we make plans for tomorrow? I'll call you in the morning, okay?"

Sue was devastated. She had hoped to have Roger to herself during his brief stay. She feared that he was going to spend the night with his young friend. The thought of it drove her crazy.

Sue went home, thinking of nothing but Roger and the young brunette. She examined herself from head to toe in the bathroom mirror. Of course, Roger wasn't going to be interested in her. There was no way that she could compete with someone almost half her age!

She conditioned her hair, exfoliated her skin and painted her nails. She wanted to look her best for Roger's last day.

Sleep was unattainable as Sue's mind wandered to what Roger and his friend might be doing.

Chapter 72

The same enzymes that digest your food while you are
alive will start eating your body once you're dead.

Roger called about nine the next morning. Sue was
agitated.

"Hi," he said, trying to sound relaxed.

"Hi," she responded plainly.

"What would you like to do today?" he asked.

"I don't know," Sue said.

"I had an idea," Roger said, "The spa here is supposed to
be world class. Want to spend the day getting pampered?"

Sue's face lit up. "That sounds wonderful. We need a
day off from riding," she added.

"Great. I'll book the appointments. Why don't you come
over about noon? We can work out in the gym and spend
the afternoon being pampered, then maybe finish up with

dinner here at one of the restaurants. Sound good?" he asked.

"It sounds perfect," Sue responded honestly.

Sue put on her skin tight, black workout pants that accentuated the roundness of her buttocks from all of the hours on a bike. She chose a hot pink top that showed a little cleavage.

She packed a gym bag with a change of clothes for dinner, her favorite pink sweat suit, a bathing suit and makeup.

Roger was waiting at the gym when Sue arrived. He was warming up on the bike.

"Some weights?" he asked.

"Sounds perfect," she answered.

Sue pulled her well-worn, lifting gloves out of her bag.

"We've been working our legs pretty hard. Want to do upper body?" she asked.

Roger was impressed. "I'll follow your lead," he said.

Sue led Roger around the gym like a pro. They worked their chests, shoulders, backs and arms.

Sue hadn't worked out with a man since Mark, and she recalled how much she had enjoyed it.

"Our first spa treatment is at 2:00," Roger said. "Why don't you take a shower and meet me in the spa lounge. I've ordered a little post-workout snack for us," he said.

"That was very thoughtful of you, Roger. I'll see you shortly," she said.

Sue met Roger in the lounge wearing a white robe and spa slippers. Roger was sitting in the lounge next to a plate of fruit and cheese. There were two large bottles of sparkling water.

"You know how to do it up right," Sue commented.

The two enjoyed the mid-afternoon snack.

"Sue, your facial appointment is ready. Please follow me," a woman instructed Sue.

"See you back here in a few hours," Roger said.

Chapter 73

A baby cannot taste salt until it is 4 months old. The delay may be related to the development of the kidneys, which start to process sodium at about that age.

Sue had a facial, massage, a scalp treatment and a pedicure. She passed a relaxing half hour in the infrared hot sauna. She felt relaxed and clean.

She put on her simple, black one-piece swimsuit and went to join Roger in the hot tub. Her body had definitely aged and she hoped that Roger would not be too disappointed when he saw her in a swimsuit.

She held her breath as she entered the tiled room. The odor of chlorine was overwhelming. Roger was already in the tub. She was wrapped in her white, spa robe. She took a deep breath as she quickly removed her robe and hung it on the hook. She entered the tub as quickly as possible. Roger smiled and scooted over to make room for her.

"How were you spa treatments?" he asked.

"Incredible. How were yours?"

"The same. I'll be going home feeling like a new person," he said.

Sue wished that he hadn't mentioned going home.

The two chatted about their day.

"I want to thank you, Sue," Roger said.

"For what?" Sue asked.

"For spending time with me over the last few days. I've thoroughly enjoyed your company," he said as he took Sue's hand.

Sue was caught by surprise as Roger leaned in to kiss her. She was even more caught off guard by the intensity of his passion. They made out in the large tub, Roger embracing Sue and exploring her steamy skin. The passion mounted until they were interrupted by a stranger entering the room.

The couple quickly stopped their embrace and Roger immediately made small talk.

"We have reservations at eight," he said. "Maybe we should shower, dress and have time for a drink before dinner."

"Great idea," Sue agreed.

They quickly made their way out of the large tub.

Chapter 74

The inner ear is the only sense organ to develop fully before birth. It reaches its adult size by the middle of pregnancy.

Sue showered and put on her favorite bright red dress. She blew her shoulder length hair straight and put on her favorite red lipstick. She wore her highest black sandals. She didn't look thirty, she concluded, but she was in better shape than anyone she knew at her age.

Roger was waiting at the table with two martinis sitting in front of him.

"I hope you don't mind," he said. "I took the liberty of ordering a martini for you."

"Thank you," Sue said, "I do like a martini from time-to-time."

"Me too," he said, "especially with a steak."

Sue felt very comfortable with Roger. She searched his steel gray eyes, trying to find a clue as to what he was thinking.

"I want to thank you again, Sue, for spending so much time with me and making me feel so comfortable."

Comfortable? That's not what she wanted to hear! Sue studied his face some more.

"Do you mind if I ask you a question?" she asked.

"Sure, what is it?" he asked.

"How old are you?"

"I'm fifty-one," he said.

Fifty-one! That was seven years younger than she. He was never going to want to be with someone that much older!

"Why do you ask?" Roger was too much of a gentleman to ask Sue her age.

"Oh, I was just wondering, that's all." Sue quickly changed the subject.

She didn't want to think about the fact that Roger was leaving and she had no idea if and when she would see him again.

They enjoyed a leisurely and relaxed dinner. Chatting superficially about world events. There was no mention of the future or future plans to see one another. Sue was developing a pit in her stomach.

"Please tell your daughter that I'm sorry I missed her," he said, "and please give her my best when you talk to her."

"I will and I'm sure that she will be surprised that you were here!" Sue had definitely been surprised!

They finished their meal and Roger offered to walk Sue to valet parking to get her car. They waited several minutes while the valet ran across the street to fetch Sue's gray SUV. She waited and wished that Roger would say something about future plans. He didn't.

The car arrived and Roger opened the door for Sue.

"Safe travels," she said and she drove off toward home.

Chapter 75

The youngest person ever to give birth was a five-year-old Peruvian girl.

Sue had a difficult few days after Roger's departure. She wondered if she would ever hear from him again.

She also wondered if he had kissed her in the hot tub in pity. Certainly if he had had a thirty-year-old girlfriend, he would not be interested in Sue. She recalled the feeling of being young and having a perfect body. Maybe Roger would truly want her if she were young again.

She knew that she truly loved him and would do anything to be with him. She just didn't know how he felt about her.

With the absence of Roger, Sue settled back into her routine. She passed her time staying as busy and distracted as possible.

She taught her spin classes, rode her bike with Margie and Kevin.

One day turned into the next. There was no word from Roger. She had to accept that she might never see him again. She held back the tears every time that she thought about him. He could have been her perfect love, if only…

It was a cold Saturday afternoon. Sue had taught spin class and was home doing laundry when the doorbell rang.

She opened the door and no one was there. She looked down to see a large brown box with a simple white label. Curious, she picked it up.

Sue carried the box into her modest kitchen, placing it on the large antique wood table. She retrieved a small knife out of her knife block and began cutting the numerous layers of tape.

Standing over the box, she could see many layers of bubble wrap with a hand-written note on top.

Sue,

As promised, here is a year's supply of the product. You will receive a similar box each year for the next 67 years as long as you keep quiet. I wish you a very long, healthy and happy life Sue. Sorry for the delay. It won't happen again.

Dr. Elmhurst

Sue quickly took a seat in one of her antique wood and leather kitchen chairs. She sat, dumbfounded, staring at the open box.

She walked to her sink and poured a large glass of water. She returned to the table, placing the glass in front of her. Sue slowly unwrapped the layers of bubble wrap and carefully opened one of the dozen plastic bottles inside.

Slowly, she took the knife and broke the seal. She removed one pill from the bottle and held it in her hand, staring at it.

She placed the pill in front of her, staring at it some more. She thought about Roger, and about Randy. She recalled everything that she had experienced while on the product.

She picked up the pill with one hand and the glass of water with the other.

Sue was startled by the sound of her cell phone ringing. She quickly put down the water and the pill on her kitchen table.

"Hello," she said, surprised.

"Hi, Sue, it's me, Roger."

About Saylor Storm

Saylor Storm is a romance author/editor of several non-fiction books. Visit Saylor online at http:// saylorstorm.com/ to find out more about the author.

You can find additional books by Saylor Storm at http:// www.amazon.com/Saylor-Storm/e/B00C8BINAI or follow her on Twitter @SaylorStorm and Facebook at https:// www.facebook.com/saylor.storm

If you enjoyed this book, please take the time to recommend it to other purchasers with a review or star rating via your retailer.

Thanks.